Red River Days

Texas Tales Book 2

A. K. Vyas

Copyright © 2023 by Aashish K. Vyas

All rights reserved. No portion of this book may be reproduced or used in any manner without written permission of the copyright owner except as permitted by U.S. copywrite law.

FIRST EDITION

www.akvyas.com

For Sean, Megan, Hannah, Clare and Alice

"The Texan turned out to be good-natured, generous and likable. In three days no one could stand him."
- Joseph Heller

"You don't just move to Texas. It moves into you."
- Manny Fernandez

CONTENTS

Preface

TEXAS IS MAGICAL.

Just about anywhere in the world, if you mention you grew up in the Lone Star State, folks smile and ask about cowboys, six guns, football and oil.

Some of my earliest memories were sitting on my dad's lap watching Cowboys games and him pointing out Roger Staubach as a true American hero. I recall scrambling for candy from the floats of the San Antonio River Parade, and the magnificent peacocks at Fort Sam Houston. There's also more than one picture of me, in a Davy Crockett hat, by a cannon at the Alamo. I still have family and close friends in Texas.

Texas underwent great change. It was part of Mexico, then an independent republic before joining the United States. The fantastic wealth from oil changed everything as well.

America herself is continuously evolving and changing. Human nature, however, is timeless. Our ancestors back in the day had similar hopes, dreams, laughter, fears and triumphs. I trust these stories are entertaining and reflect both the beauty and frailties of the human condition.

After my father, Roger Staubach is still a hero to me.

We need heroes and heroines in life.

Any of these stories can be read as standalones. They all describe the wanderings of an intrepid cowboy, Wade Maverick, across the vast world of 19th-century Texas.

I trust you'll enjoy *Texas Tales*.

PARADISE LOST
PARADISE TALE

"A faint heart never filled a flush."
— **Kansas Proverb**

19th Century Texas

THERE'S A DRIED STRETCHED rattlesnake skin over the cantle of my saddle.

The old vaqueros believed this brought good luck and cured rheumatism. I still get sore and it wasn't very lucky for the snake. There ain't much logic to it, I suppose, since no man wants any part of a diamondback between his legs.

Old habits die hard.

Then again, old cowhands didn't get old by accident—maybe they knew something.

Badger and I had left Fort Worth about eight that morning. It was a crisp gray day with a nip of chill to the air. Badger felt it too and wanted to lope faster than the trot I was holding him to. A good horse is like family, they usually know what's right for you, but I had to rein him in that day or we would have missed the trail to Paradise.

Paradise is a dusty speck of a town about five miles past the western fork of the Trinity River. They used to call it El Dorado, then they figured out a bunch of places were named that, so they renamed the town Paradise Prairie. Now it's just Paradise.

Will Anderson ran the general store there, and he was good people. He'd been a lumberjack in Minnesota and decided broiling Texas heat beat bone-chilling northern snow. I'd bought a lasso from him which broke the next day. Will was kind enough to replace it for free. The town was growing fast, it even had a post office now.

I remembered all of this while Badger was drinking his fill from the river maybe three hours before dusk. I scratched behind his ears but wasn't able to stretch the saddle stiffness out of myself.

As I said, old habits die hard.

I always send a letter to my old aunt Betsie before leaving for a roundup, and I'd forgotten to mail it this morning. So, the notion of dropping by the Paradise post office and catching up with Will over a whiskey made perfect sense. I figured to stay overnight then ride on toward the roundup in Lubbock the next day.

The lack of sun gave way to low creeping fog as darkness approached. The town had fresh paint on the church, and a new warehouse since I last came through.

There was only the one street and it was deserted except for scraggly tumbleweed rolling lazily in the wind.

That's peculiar.

Now Paradise wasn't so big. It had maybe sixty or so folks living there, but there wasn't a soul to be seen.

A pair of saddled horses were wandering riderless just past where the street ended. They whinnied, jerked their heads and ran off.

What? This isn't right.

I tied Badger to the saddle post outside the post office. The door was wide open and once inside I saw a safe was sitting there open as well.

Something's wrong.

Then Badger snorted and shied at the post. I thought I heard something faint flittering in the wind.

Was that a baby crying?

I thought, *Maybe it's some local holiday and everyone's at church or in the saloon.*

Saloon's closer.

In Texas, it's always better to check the saloon first.

I saw nary a soul through the side windows, which struck me as odd. There was a new sidewalk since my last time through. Years under that steaming Texas sun and arid winds had already warped and splintered its tobacco-stained planks.

There's always someone in a saloon. Sometimes they brought both their guns and their dogs with them as well.

It's Texas after all.

The faded red saloon doors were about a hundred feet toward the end of Main Street.

I never got there.

The all too familiar click of a shotgun cocked just behind me as I passed the stables.

"Reach for the sky or die! Now, hands up. You move, we blast!"

I felt a hand remove my pistol from behind, then shove me forward.

"All right mister, now turn around real slow like."

Then, I realized what had slithered in to Paradise.

There were three of them and they were killers. A man gets to know that look in the eye of a killer, and you're lucky if you see it in time to do something before it's too late. They were all covered in dust with two-week beards, but their pistols were shining and their holsters unsoiled.

Their leader was a sallow, bacon-thin little man on the gray side of sixty. His pinched blue eyes were turbulent and cruel.

One of them held up my Colt. "Look at this boss, a fancy red grip."

The old man twitched then scowled at me. "What's your name, mister?"

"Maverick, Wade Maverick."

"The Red Gun? Naw, it can't be."

One of them sneered, "Maybe it is?"

"Let's just blast him now, boss, either way."

"Hobble your lips! The both of you," said the old man. "Let me think on this."

This one's as touchy as a sore-footed badger.

"Are all them stories about you true?"

I just shrugged.

A wicked glint came over those old blue eyes. "Maverick, huh? A bona fide sheepdog if ever I saw one. Maybe them sheep will bleat for you?"

What is this crazy windbag rambling on about?

"How's that?"

"You see, Maverick there's only three types of people."

"Oh?"

"Yup, wolves, sheep, and sheepdogs."

"What?"

"Most folks are sheep. They're stupid pack animals without a shred of backbone and born to be fleeced. Then there's wolves. We feed on the sheep and just take what we want. The worst of the lot is sheepdogs. Men with teeth like wolves who are fool enough to guard the sheep when they could be eating them too. Men too stupid to see the sheep aren't worth it.... Men like you."

"I see."

"No, you don't. That's the problem. My boys are right we should just blast you, but them sheep trust the damn sheepdogs. You just might be able get me what I want."

"Is that right?"

One of the gang sneered, "I doubt it. Let's just gun him."

The old man just held up my pistol. "Pipe down, boys. Without this, you watch, he'll be on his belly begging like the rest of them. Take him to the warehouse."

ᘮᘮᘮᘮᘮᘮᘮᘮ

The folks who lived in Paradise were all inside the warehouse. There were also four more wild-eyed men leaning against the wall near the door guarding them. These outlaws glared at me with guns held lazily in their hands.

They've taken over the whole town for some reason, but why?

My eyes were drawn to a slender woman of thirty who looked forty.

She was trying to calm a red-faced fussing baby. I'd forgotten her name. The fear in her tired hazel eyes was palpable.

Frontier life will do that to you.

Days like this don't help...

An outlaw grunted, "Lady, if you don't shut that kid up, I'll do it for you!"

She was shaking as she held the baby to her chest and moved to the back wall. Her baby boy sensed her fear as well. Somehow she managed to soothe him as only mothers can.

I fought down the anger welling up. It's hard for men to see womenfolk and babies being terrified.

There were a number of familiar faces among the captives, and I nodded to Will Anderson. He was right in the middle of the crowd toward the back wall, and I sensed they were looking to him for leadership and strength.

I was slowly making my way over to talk to Will when the warehouse doors slammed open again. The late amber sunlight revealed the wild-eyed old man flanked by the two killers from earlier. He ordered our four guards to go eat and looked over at me.

The old man was red-faced and shaking like a man possessed.

"You, Maverick, maybe you can help save these people. There's a bastard in this room that killed my son. These fools won't give him up. I want that man. Maybe they'll listen to you. Otherwise...It's gonna get so there is a lot more killing around here. Talk to them for a couple of minutes, but don't no man try anything stupid. We're just outside."

They slammed and locked the door behind them on the way out.

Will came over and we shook.

I asked, "A holdup gone bad?"

"Yeah, Wade. They rode in early this morning. Ten men. The Whitley Gang I reckon."

"Brack Whitley?"

Will nodded.

So, the old gray hair is Brack Whitley. A gang of bloodthirsty bank robbers who were wanted in four states.

"I figured them for trouble. They come in to the store and a bunch of them knocked me down at gunpoint. The others grabbed two women hostages. Whitley was cleaning out the safe when a handful of local men saw what was happening and started shooting. They shot a few of the bastards down in front of my store, and more Paradise men came runnin' over with guns.... But then, Whitley and his boys came outside with guns to the heads of the two women hostages and threated to kill every woman in town unless we dropped our guns."

I nodded. "Then what?"

"Well, four local men were shot dead but we'd shot down three of them. One we'd killed was Whitley's son. Whitley went crazy demanding to know who did it. He had his outfit round up a couple more women and swore he'd kill all the women and burn Paradise down. Then he was damn near foaming at the mouth as he murdered the three local men standing closest to the store. They've kept us all locked up in here, since then."

"Yeah."

"I reckon we gave up too easy. We just didn't want no women shot. Anyway, in Whitley's mind, his son's been murdered. He says he'll take us out a few at a time and shoot until we tell him."

I nodded.

A lean oval-faced man in a torn farmer's shirt spoke up. "The thing is mister, it all happened so fast with all the shooting we don't know who killed Whitley's son. I'm Yaro Brock and I got a place just outside of town."

"Yeah."

"That's my wife over there with the baby. Listen, we all gotta do something quick before they kill us all!"

"Take it easy."

"No! We're running out of time. There's near twenty men in here. We could rush them. Some of us will die, but otherwise they'll kill us all. It's our only chance."

The clanging of chains being removed outside the door silenced us.

Whitley and two of his gang stepped inside with guns leveled at us.

"All right, what do you got to tell me? Maverick, come over here, what do you got to say?"

"I don't know. It seems to me you broke the law by robbing the store. It's the chance your son, a fully grown man, took for being a part of a holdup."

"He was shot in the back!" roared Whitley.

"I wasn't there. Gunplay is what it is. Everyone's moving, it's all fast and confusing like, maybe he turned around looking to kill a man himself."

Whitley's eyes fired up. "I ain't bluffing! I'll wipe out this whole stinking town! ...I'll do it!"

"That still doesn't get your son back. It's one thing to rob a train, but are you gonna start the habit of butchering women and kids?"

"Shut your trap! I'll show you my mind."

Whitley pointed at Yaro Brock and another man. "You two come with us."

Mrs. Brock's panicked eyes pleaded no as the outlaws moved toward her husband.

It happened in a blur.

Yaro Brock snapped.

He lunged screaming bloody murder for Whitley's throat. They shot him down like a feral dog.

The women were shaking and sobbing and I saw men's fists ball up white-knuckled.

Whitley growled. "That fellow don't count no more! Now is someone gonna tell me who killed my boy? ...No? ...Fine, have it your way. We still need two men."

They kept us covered while Whitely pointed his pistol at another fellow in the room.

"You, you're gonna take his place. Come with us."

Will said, "Whitley, they won't just hang you for doing this, they will burn you at the stake."

"That'll be the day."

They took both men outside with them and locked us in again.

They left us all watching the dark lifeblood pooling out of Brock's body while his wife sobbed over it.

ʊʊʊʊʊʊʊ

Half an hour passed in nervous silence. Maybe the killers didn't come back right away because they didn't have the nerve to face up for what they'd done.

We'll never know.

We eventually heard two shots echo from down the street.

Either way, no choice now.

We whispered amongst ourselves. Two local men who'd shot at the gang where willing to give themselves up to save everyone but another two weren't, and who could blame them. Will Anderson and I posted a lookout at the window and tried to come up with some sort of plan in the corner.

The early evening air wafted through the windows, adding its chill to the tension in the warehouse.

Will said, "They won't stop. Maybe they need to liquor up some before they come back. It's up to us. It'll be night soon and no one's gonna ride by to help. I don't want to hear another woman cry like that. We got to fight now."

"Yeah."

The lookout whispered, "They're coming back, two of them."

"All right, get away from that window," I said. "Three of you stand to the other side of the door by Will. Then you two with me on this side. We wait until they're inside and have closed the door behind them. We'll give them a second to relax, then grab them fast. Go when you see me go. We'll stomp them on the ground. We can't let them yell or shoot...Got it, boys?"

Grim, determined faces nodded back at me.

"Everybody quiet now."

A man asked, "What if there's more behind these two?"

"No choice," Will answered.

Then we went silent and were waiting inside to jump them. We could hear the two outlaws outside fumbling with the padlock on the door. One of them belched as the stale stench of whiskey breath wafted inside.

What came next froze our blood.

It started with a gravelly voice from just outside. "Hold up a minute, Curly. I gots me an idea."

"Yeah?"

"Boss is going about this all wrong. We need to get out of this fleabag town before someone rides by and sees us."

"Whitley won't leave until we settle scores for his boy."

The response was a sinister cackle. "Yup, but have you noticed these here men are mighty soft on their womenfolk? There's that one woman in there, the pretty perky-titted little one."

"Well, now I'll be. Yeah, the towheaded young one, I'd sure like a romp in her melon patch. I bet she's good and tight."

"Yup, so the way I see it, let's just take her out of there. Maybe that'll finally get them to talk, and boss lets us leave. Hell, I reckon we'll have a heap of fun either way..."

Everyone waiting inside heard all of this.

Every word.

The young teenaged blonde in the warehouse put her hand over her mouth and began sobbing and quaking in fear. A room full of arms were quick to hug and comfort her.

I watched cold, murderous primal rage seep into the eyes of every man inside the warehouse.

"It'll be all right, Klara." Will looked her in the eyes and whispered, "We won't let them."

No matter what happens.

We're going to tear these two apart.

No matter what goes down.

These two die.

The door finally creaked open and they stepped inside with guns drawn. One of them was husky, bearded and swarthy and the other was a callow, thin ferret-faced fellow. Both leered at Klara in the back of the room.

The door closed behind them as the big fellow said, "You, miss, you need to come with us. We won't hurt you and want to talk to you outside..."

The flickering lamp light reflected on his thin wicked smile.

He never finished his sentence since Will's massive lumberjack fist caught him right under the ear, as I poked the skinny one in the eye and slammed my forearm down on his bony wrist. This knocked his gun away as the man next to me grabbed him over the mouth.

A room full of enraged, desperate men got them two to the ground and stomped, tore and kicked them down like a vengeful pack of timber wolves taking down a moose.

The big one had two pistols on him, while the little one had a gun and a knife.

I took a pistol and offered one to Will.

"Give me the knife, Wade. I'm not a great shot."

"All right, which two of you men are the best shots?"

Two hands went up. I handed them the other two pistols and we split up the cartridges.

"Now what?" Will asked.

"Well, I didn't think we'd get this far."

That was good for a few dark grins.

I added, "Okay, there's only five of them left now. Us three will go after the rest of them. Will, I reckon you stay here, with the knife, in case more come back."

Will shook his head. "No, we need to leave a man with a gun behind, to at least have some defense here for all these folks. Ted, you stay behind and shoot to kill. Jimmy and I'll go with Wade."

"That knife won't do much good in a gunfight."

"Yeah," Will responded. "I reckon that axe is still in the stump by the woodshed just outside. I'm good with an axe."

There was no time to argue.

We three slipped outside and that axe was just where Will said it would be. They'd left the bodies of the two men they'd murdered earlier just lying there off Main Street. There was a mangy dog whimpering over them in the dust.

We waited a bit to listen and watch.

Several men could be heard inside the saloon.

It surely helped the sun was setting as we crept to the side of the saloon, ducking down below the windows. They'd left a man guarding the back door to the saloon. That made sense since he could watch the main trail into town from there.

I crawled to the corner of the saloon and peeked around the corner. The guard was sitting lazily in a rocking chair with a shotgun in his lap.

I turned back to Will and Jimmy and whispered.

"One guard sitting by the door with a shotgun. I'll shoot him, then we rush in through the back door blasting away. Will, take his shotgun. You come up the middle, just point and shoot. Two blasts of buckshot up close is no joke. Jimmy and I will be on either side of you with the pistols. All right?"

"Wade, they'll hear you shoot the guard and be waiting for us."

"No choice, it won't be long before they check the warehouse again."

"I can split that man down with this axe."

"It's ten yards to him, he'll see you before you can get close enough."

"Trust me. I can make that throw."

I saw Will's big Minnesota lumberjack fist tightening around the axe handle.

He wasn't a man to bet against.

We charged around the corner with Will in the lead.

He took a big step and reared up with a powerful cast.

This outlaw had no chance.

That guard spent the rest of his life staring at a big old axe whirling for him end over end as the blade caught sunset's final gleam of light. He had no time to grab for the shotgun and barely got his hands up to shield his face as the blade slammed in right between his eyes. The impact knocked both him and the chair over in a dusty thud that sounded and looked like a shattered jar of red jam.

Four left.

We were on him in a flash but he was deader than a doornail. I handed Will his shotgun and reminded him he only had two barrels.

We came in fast and furious, blasting away through the back door, and gave them no chance.

All four of them were huddled around a table playing poker with a whiskey bottle.

Nothing can clear a room up close like a scattergun point blank. Jimmy and I emptied our pistols into them from either side of Will.

The poker table tipped over as the room erupted into a whirlwind of screams, blood, smoke and shattered glass.

It was over in a blink.

Not one of them even got a hand on a gun.

The old man's hissed breathing was the only sound in the gore splattered saloon.

I put Whitley's pistol in my belt as he bled from a bullet in each shoulder and propped him up in a chair.

"Y'all killed my boy," he spat out, wheezing a glob of foaming pink blood.

"You'll see him in Hell," Jimmy snickered.

Those old cruel eyes closed with a gasping rattle.

"The old devil's still breathing." Jimmy declared.

Will dropped the smoking shotgun on a table and walked outside. I followed him into the cold night air and saw he was holding on to a wooden post on the sidewalk and bent over retching into the dark earth.

"You good?"

"I thought we was dead for sure."

"Me too."

"Wade, I...I...been throwing axes at trees and boards since I was in short pants...I ...I never had a day like today...I never killed no one before."

I put an arm on his shoulder.

"It's rough. You know things could have gone down much worse, but not for you and that axe?"

"Yeah."

"You good, Will?"

"Yeah, I reckon I just needed a minute. How about you, Wade?"

"Well, do you recall what them two sidewinders we beat down were saying they were fixing to do to that young lady?"

"Yeah."

"They meant it."

"Yeah, so what's next?"

"Well, remind me to never rein in Badger again when he wants to lope past a town."

Will gave a baleful bellow.

There isn't much more to tell. Paradise recovered just fine, though life would never be the same for those who lost kin, and especially those poor women who lost their men to the Whitley Gang.

Somehow, Brack Whitley, the worst of the lot, was the only one to survive a brace of pistols and buckshot close up. I remember when the jury tried him in a packed Wise County courtroom.

I was there when they hanged him.

Starlit Twirl
Nacogdoches Tale

"The best sermons are lived, not preached."
– Louisiana Proverb

E AST TEXAS IS LUSH, green and magical. Maybe because it borders Louisiana with all that New Orleans legends and lore. It's certainly nothing like that red desert caliche that springs to mind when folks mention Texas.

It was maybe six o'clock on a Saturday evening as Badger and I took the east trail leading from Nacogdoches over to McFarland Ranch. Any part of this big old state is still that same sun-warmed Texas soil. Which is another way of saying it was so hot, the trees were bribing the dogs.

A little breeze was flaring up now, hinting at nightfall cooling things down some. That isn't always a given in these parts—sometimes that sticky heat just lingers past the light.

Twilight was about the only thing on the horizon. It's amazing what you can see when you aren't looking.

I hadn't seen any signs of habitation for the last few miles. The trail meandered lazily around an apple grove. A truly magnificent eighteen-point buck was just standing in the middle of the trail and barely acknowledged me.

Either he figures it's too hot to hunt, or somehow he just knows I haven't been able to shoot a deer since I was a boy.

The soil here was dark and rich with verdant foliage. I noticed a gray stone house sitting back roughly sixty yards off the trail. When I was almost flush with the house, the front door opened and a lithe young boy came sprinting out toward me. "Hey there! Howdy mister, could you hold up a minute, please?"

He looked like he was about fifteen, wearing torn blue jeans, a checkered red shirt and a little peaked cap pulled down tight over his ears.

"Whoa Badger, whoa boy, whoa Badger. Howdy son, how can I help?"

"You come from Nacogdoches, mister?"

"I did."

"You didn't run across Derek Faulk on the trail, did you?"

"Derek Faulk?"

Everyone knows him, mister. He runs that big traveling mercantile wagon."

"A mercantile cart?"

"Yup, we're too far out to get into town very much so he brings around a wagon full of goods every once so often. I just don't know how we'd cope so well without him."

A shrill woman's voice called out from inside the house. "Well, don't stand out there all flapping your gums! Just find out about Derek like I told you!"

The boy yelled back to the house, "The gentleman ain't seen him, ma'am."

The woman yelled back through the window, "Fine! Then shut the fence and you get back here! The supper dish is a-waiting, Cyndi-Jo."

I asked, "What was that she called you?"

"Cyndi-Jo."

"That's a girl's name. Oh, oh no, in this light here, the way you were dressed, I'm sorry,

I sort of thought maybe you were."

"It don't matter so much. Thanks again, mister. So long."

"Yeah, so long so long, Cyndi-Jo."

Well, I gave Badger a touch of my heel. "Let's go, come on. Come on boy." He started a brisk trot. I figured I had about ten miles to go until I reached the McFarland Ranch. I hadn't been through this part of the country going on three years but I was pretty certain the owner, George Ella, remembered me from back in the day. He'd always signed me on for the summer if he had an opening.

"Come on Badger, come on, come on. Let's not be late."

Then I came across a fork in the trail. I saw a massive wagon rolling along from the south. It was as big as a small house. I'd never run into anything that size on wheels before. The canvas bulged out, it looked like it was loaded to the hilt. I had a hunch this was that mercantile wagon Cyndi-Jo had asked about.

"Whoa there, boy. Howdy, you're Mr. Faulk I take it."

"You got that right, sir, except just call me Derek like everyone does. A friend

in need is a friend indeed. Something you needing, mister?"

"No, I'm fine."

"I got it all here. Shoelaces, kettles, salt, knives, ammunition, hats, smoking tobacco, anything at all. If you can name it, I got it here in my wagon."

"I believe that."

"That's only a part of it. I didn't even touch on my medical supplies. Well, what about work clothes? I've got a full line of them fancy new California style Levi's pants, shirts, bandanas, and good straw hats for this infernal heat."

"No, I'm afraid I'm just not needing to buy much of anything, Derek. The real reason I stopped was to share those folks down the trail were anxious to see you."

"Folks down the trail?"

"Yes, a stone house a couple miles back toward Nacogdoches."

"I surely can't recall who you're talking about, mister. I ain't even headed that way. I'm making a delivery over the Jordan

Ranch near San Augustine. Jordan's girl's getting hitched tomorrow morning. I'm bringing a whole mess of fancy dresses for the wedding. You sure somebody around these parts is looking for me?"

"I don't actually know the family's name. The girl asking if I seen you was called Cyndi-Jo."

He smiled at the mention of the name.

"That would be young Miss Cyndi-Jo Stroud. But why would... Oh Nellie! Helen Stroud! I owe her that dress she ordered for her daughter Sarah. What time you make it out to be, mister? I ain't unpacked my shipment of alarm clocks yet."

"I'd say 7:30."

"Well, maybe I can get there before they leave. If I don't, Helen Stroud will tan my hide. Dang it! I knew there was something else, and I was working on that dress only this morning. So long mister. Hope you enjoy the square dance."

"Dance? What dance?"

"That's where you're heading, ain't it? McFarland Ranch?"

"Yeah, as a matter of fact it is, but I didn't know about any dance. I was going to ask George Ella for a job."

"There ain't no way you ain't heard about the festivities tonight?"

"No, I hadn't."

"George Ella's son has just come home from school back east."

"What, you mean little Tommy Ella?"

"Yeah, that's the boy's name. You know him, mister?"

"Well, I used to. He was just a little button then."

"It's just Tom now, and he's a strapping twenty-year-old college man. I reckon he'll be taking over the crown one of these days."

"I reckon my job hunting can wait a spell. I wouldn't want to bother George Ella at the party. I'll ride along with you a bit though."

Well, if you're an acquaintance of George Ella's, I'd bet you're more than welcome at his party. In fact the whole county has been invited."

"Maybe so, maybe so, but fact is I'm not so much for square dancing."

"Well, I just hope you're the only absentee."

"How's that?"

"Well, Helen Stroud's daughter Sarah was planning to wear this here dress tomorrow. They special ordered it from me."

"Oh. yeah?"

"Sarah's got a temper just like her ma. I bet she's pitching a biblical hissy fit right about now!"

"She can still go to the dance, can't she?"

"Well, yes, but there's hell to pay because Helen has designs on marrying her Sarah off to Tom Ella. This special dress was intended to make Sarah shine tonight. Helen is what they call a battleaxe. She usually gets what she wants, otherwise watch out. She's going to be awful sore at me for forgetting."

"Well, none of that's my business. I hope everyone enjoys the dance. It looks like folks are headed that way." I pointed to a buggy coming over a hill and down the trail.

"Oh my gracious! That's Helen and Sarah. I know their buggy! It's too late to get them the dress now. I best get out of sight. Excuse me, I best get this here wagon under them trees over there!"

"But, ah, Derek they're bound to see your wagon sitting there."

"You don't know Helen Stroud like I do. She's a hellcat if I ever saw one, but she's also as near-sighted as a bat. Thank the lord!"

"I don't think bats are near-sighted."

"It don't matter! She can't see her hand in front of her face unless she's wearing her bifocals!"

"But she'd wear them to drive the buggy?"

"Friend, you don't know much about lady folk, they never wear glasses to a dance."

He spurred his horses and made for the cover of a nearby weeping willow grove.

"Won't the daughter see you?"

He looked back and yelled over the crunch of his wagon wheels. "No, Sarah takes after her mama in more ways than one. She's as blind as a bat too!.... Hey, could you please ride over here and wait under this tree with me until they pass...Please, them seeing you might lead them to see me!"

"Derek, they will pass within twenty yards of us, I mean…"

"Please!"

I laughed and moseyed Badger over next to the wagon.

He was right, by golly.

They passed us by without so much as a glance!

They weren't ugly women either but had such fierce scowls on their faces that Derek's hiding now made perfect sense.

"What did I tell you?" Derek giggled. "They missed us!"

"You were right…. Well, I reckon it's high time for me to ride on. Nice meeting you, Derek."

"Nice meeting you too, mister."

"Oh, my apologies, Derek. I meant to introduce myself. My name's Maverick, Wade Maverick."

"The Red Gun?"

"Uh, yeah."

"I didn't recognize you."

"Well, no reason why you should, Derek."

"Well, I heard so much about you. Maybe I'm a tad nearsighted as well for missing that red pearl handle in your holster. Well I best get going myself. Here is a free bottle of New Orleans shaving soap for you. Not that there's nothing wrong with your beard, Mr. Red Gun, sir!"

"Oh, thank you. Please just call me Wade."

"My pleasure, Wade."

Then it hit me.

"Say Derek, there were only the two of them in that buggy. I'm wondering what about the other daughter?"

"Who?"

"The young lady I met back at the stone house."

"Oh, you mean Cyndi-Jo? Well, she wouldn't be going to the Ella's dance."

"But, you said the whole county was invited?"

"Helen ain't got much use for her. Cyndi-Jo ain't Helen's real kin. She's just her stepdaughter and her papa passed."

"I see."

"Yeah, Helen and Sarah, well, they just seem to go out of their way to make things miserable for her. Take this here dance, for instance. Everybody knows that Tom Ella and Cyndi-Jo used to be sweet on one another back when they was kids. Heck, she'd probably give her eye tooth to go to that shindig, come to think of it."

"Well that don't seem fair."

"Yeah, well it's too bad she can't. There's nothing to be done about it now. Why she don't even have a dress to her name."

I said, "She seemed a mighty nice looking girl to me. I reckon she's pretty as a peach if they ever allowed her to fix herself up."

Derek got a mischievous spark to his eyes.

"Wade, are you thinking what I'm thinking?"

"I believe so."

"You're right! Why shouldn't Cyndi-Jo go to that dance tonight? With all the stuff in this wagon, I could fix her up so she'd shine like an angel!"

"I believe it."

"Why didn't I think of this myself? Life may not be fair, but good men try to be.... and—" He gave a dark cackle. "It sure would be a fun trick to play on Helen and Sarah. Even if there's hell to pay afterwards."

"I dunno, Derek. I reckon they passed within spitting distance of your wagon and missed us, so they won't recognize Cyndi-Jo in a nice dress."

"Yup, but a girl can't go to square dance all by herself. She's got to have an escort.... Wade."

Oh, I suppose so, but... Oh, now hold your horses, there. You don't mean...?"

"I do, You're a friend of the Ellas, you said so yourself. If we don't hurry, Wade, the square dance will be all over. There ain't no other option."

"Why, I'm old enough to be her father?"

"Look man, all you go to do is walk her in on your shoulder, mosey over by Tommy, maybe do one dance with her, then let them two be. Heck, then you could likely just sit back and have some whiskeys until it's time to escort her back."

"I don't know about this."

"Let's fly!"

∪∪∪∪∪∪∪

We got back to the old stone house right fast.

Cyndi-Jo was thankful but flat refused to go.

"I just don't get it, Derek. You mean to loan me a dress?"

"With all the trimmings! Cyndi-Jo before I get done with you, you'll be so duded up that your own stepmother won't recognize you."

"And you want to take me to the dance, Mr. Maverick?"

"I do. That is, if you want to go."

"Well, that's right kindly of you both, but the fact is, I haven't a shred of interest in attending square dances at the McFarlands'."

I shrugged. "Oh, you don't? Well, in that case..."

"Derek, I don't know where you ever got such a notion. As if I cared anything about seeing Tom Ella again. I haven't even thought of him since he went away back east. Not once!"

Derek narrowed his eyes. "Well, I reckon your stepsister Sarah's fixing to do something about him."

She flared. "A lot of good it'll do her... Tommy wouldn't look twice at... I mean, none of my business."

I nodded. "I reckon it is. I'm sorry we bothered you. Let's go, Derek."

"Okay, Wade."

She was of course watching us leave, when a tinge of hope caught her eyes.

"Was there something you wanted, Cyndi-Jo?"

"I guess maybe I'm acting plumb ungrateful. I mean, well, you both did put yourself out for me and it was real touching. I don't suppose it would do me no harm to go to that square dance. For a little while, anyway.... If you really want me to."

"Well, now that's more like it!"

She was positively beaming now.

Derek said, "Hmm, let's see now, the first thing we've got to do is find the right dress. You come on out to my wagon, Cyndi-Jo, we'll pick something that'll make you look like royalty. Yes, sir, a real princess."

Well, I want to tell you, Derek was spot-on.

I've never seen anything like it in all my days.

Cyndi-Jo's transformation when she finally came out of her room in that dress had us speechless.

We just stood there, just not saying a word, just staring at her.

"Wait, is something wrong? Don't I look good enough to go to the dance?"

"Good enough.? Why, Cyndi-Jo, you're prettier than a speckled pup under a wagon with his tongue hanging out!"

She looked to me.

"Young lady, you're pretty enough to make a man plow through a hickory stump!"

Derek said, "Well, if you're ready, Cyndi-Jo?"

"Uh, there's just one thing. We forgot the shoes."

"Shoes?"

"I don't have any dance slippers of my own."

"Oh, well, you see, Cyndi-Jo, that's about the only item I don't stock in my wagon."

"Well, I guess you can make do with the shoes you're wearing, can't you?"

"Oh no, I don't think that'll work. Well, I'd just look silly in these boots.."

"Yeah, hey, wait a second, I am carrying one pair of party slippers. They're part of the Jordan girls' wedding outfit...But, well, I'm sorry but I just don't know. I couldn't loan them to Cyndi-Jo, though. I've got to leave for the Jordans' ranch as soon as you two start off for the dance. I promise I'd be there first thing in the morning, and it's a good eight hours' drive on that wagon of mine."

Cyndi-Jo took it gracious. "I understand. Well, it was real nice of you both anyhow. I'll never forget what you two tried to do for me and how wonderful I felt when I put on this dress."

"Derek, what if I had her back here by midnight?"

"You know, Wade, that dog will hunt. I reckon if I could still make it to the Jordans' place by eight o'clock, but you can't be late, all right?"

"There ain't no reason why we couldn't both couldn't be back here in time."

"I reckon so, of course we don't even know if them slippers will fit, I'll got fetch them."

She watched him head for the wagon. "I just truly don't know what to say, Mr. Maverick. I've never even dreamed of something like this ever happening to me. It all seems like something out of a storybook."

"You know, Cyndi-Jo, I was thinking just that."

"Here you go, Cyndi-Jo. Try them on. Gee, they sure do look a mite small, don't they? Hmm. You think you can make it?"

"Oh, I don't... Oh, there. Oh, it's kind of tight, but I... "

"Time's a wasting, girl, try the other one!"

She got them on.

"There now, good. Now, are you going to be able to walk?"

"Oh, I'll be able to walk all right, Derek. The way I feel right now, I can almost fly!"

Well, get going, you two. You don't have too long to the dance, you know. Wade, don't forget, you've must have her back here by midnight, or my goose is cooked. It's a full forty minute ride both ways."

"You have my word, Derek."

Well, I hoisted Cyndi-Jo up on Badger as she managed to seat herself in front of the saddle. I kind of held on to her to keep her from falling off, and we started off for McFarland Ranch.

◡◡◡◡◡◡◡

The hoedown was in full swing when we walked into the parlor.

The square dancing fest was on!

"Rope your cow and brand your calf. Bring your honey at hour and a half!"

George Ella came over to the door when he saw us and welcomed us. He was real gracious considering I'd invited myself. I sort of managed to avoid mentioning Cyndi-Jo's name, and amidst all the joyous din, George didn't seem to notice that I hadn't introduced her proper like.

But George's son, Tommy, well, he didn't wait for no introduction. That boy was thunderstruck like rain in the desert after a seven-year West Texas drought. He took just one long look at Cyndi-Jo, and that was the last I saw of her.

The other girls at the party were just completely outclassed from then on. I waited until there was an intermission and the dancing, and then realized I was mighty parched myself. I moseyed over to the punch bowl. Helen Stroud was holding court there with the ladle.

"Oh, can I help you, mister?"

"Maverick, Wade Maverick, ma'am. Thank you."

"I'm Mrs. Stroud, Helen Stroud."

"Oh, how do you, Mrs. Stroud?"

"Oh, Sarah, over here, dear. I want you to meet somebody. This is my daughter, Sarah,"

"It's a pleasure to meet you, Sarah."

"Well, speak up, speak up. Oh, she's sort of shy."

"Uh, yeah."

"Oh, by the way, Mr. Maverick, that young lady that you brought to the dance isn't spending so much time with you, is she? Oh, that's the trouble when a man brings a pretty girl to a dance. He's apt to find himself all alone some. Sarah, stop your fidgeting."

"Oh, uh."

"Of course, now, some girls have character as well as looks."

"Grab your partner and swing around next to him. Everybody join in!"

"Lordy. They're starting another dance. Now, Mr. Maverick, don't think you need to ask my permission to dance with Sarah. You just go right ahead."

"Yes, uh, uh, Miss Sarah?"

"Uh huh!"

I took her hand and off we went.

"More hand-hugs, here we go. Turn around and around and doh see do!"

Like I said, I'm not much of a square dancer. Well, I guess I should say there wasn't any way of turning Sarah's mother down. So, we did our best, my two left feet and all.

"Woops, sorry again, Sarah, is your foot okay?"

As the evening wore on, it didn't seem she had any other partners lined up. Well, I figured I was kind of obligated.

"Oh Nellie, I sure didn't mean to kick your ankle there, Sarah!"

To be fair, Sarah sure didn't talk a man to death. Truth be told it was fun, and the next thing I knew the clock had struck eleven.

I got to get Cyndi-Jo back home.

She was nowhere in sight.

I excused myself from Sarah and headed out to the front porch. Yup, Cyndi-Jo was there all right. But surprisingly she was all alone. Her eyes told me she'd been crying.

"Hey there, Cyndi-Jo."

"Oh, Mr. Maverick."

"What, are you all right?"

"Oh, I'm fine. Just fine."

"Where's Tommy?"

"I don't know."

"Well, you'd best go and say goodnight."

"I never want to see him again! Not as long as I live!"

"What happened? I thought you two was like peas and carrots?"

"I thought so, too, at first. While we were inside dancing, everything was just heaven. Then then all of a sudden he started acting like he didn't care about me at all. Tommy said he couldn't be spending all his time with one girl. He had to dance with some of the others. Well, after all, the party is in his honor. And that ain't all, Mr. Maverick."

"Oh?"

"He didn't even know who I was!"

"Well, didn't you tell him? "

I thought.... Well I never figured he'd forget me. Not in just a few years."

"Well, you've changed, Cyndi-Jo. You're a grown woman now, and you look so different all fixed up."

"That shouldn't matter...Not if Tommy really liked me. I'd never forget him. I'd know him no matter how much he changed or how he dressed."

"Why not just tell him who you were?"

"No, I just couldn't. And you mustn't tell him either. You've got to promise me you won't! Please, Mr. Maverick."

"If that's what you want. Well, I think it's time we best leave.".

"Yes, I'm ready."

"You got everything?

"I guess so. Why?"

"I don't know. I just reckoned maybe you'd lost a slipper."

"Whatever gave you that idea?"

"I don't know. The notion just sort of crossed my mind. Never mind."

Well, that just goes to show you that Texas tales in real life don't work out the same way as in the Old World. Instead of falling in love, Cyndi-Jo and Tommy Ella were just as far apart as the Grand Canyon. And there didn't seem to be any way of bridging that gulf.

Tommy surely wasn't going to be able to do it by finding one of her slippers at the dance, that's for sure. For what it's worth, she couldn't have lost a shoe at the dance if her heart was set on it. When we got her home, them slippers was plumb stuck to her feet.

I was helping steady her in a chair while Derek was tugging to get them there slippers off her feet for all he was worth.

"C'mon now, Cyndi-Jo. You must not be trying. You didn't have near as much trouble getting them on."

"I'm so sorry, Derek. I'm truly trying. My feet must have swelled up from the dancing or something."

They were just plain stuck.

"Maybe by morning my feet will go back to normal?"

I could hear a buggy approaching. "Hey, that's got to be Mrs. Stroud and Sarah."

Derek was wide-eyed. "Holy smoke. I don't want no part of them catching me neither. So long, Cyndi-Jo!"

He ran for the wagon and took up the reins.

"I'll see you, Wade. This was great fun!"

"But what about the slippers in the wedding tomorrow?"

"The bride's wearing a long dress, which is clear down to the floor. She can get married in bare feet if she has to. I got to at least get her the dress or Mr. Jordan will tan my hide hisself!"

"Well, thanks for everything!"

"Good night, Cyndi-Jo. I'm sorry things didn't work out better for you, young lady, but good night."

UUUUUUU

Well, just past noontime the following day I was in my hotel room washing up for Sunday supper. They were planning to serve fried chicken, gumbo and pecan pie. The Nacogdoches Inn always served their meals early and family style, so I figured I'd better be real prompt or risk missing out on pie.

There was an excited knock and familiar voice at my door.

"I didn't get a chance to say goodbye at the dance, Mr. Maverick."

"Oh, hello Tom."

"What are you doing in town? I've been looking for you all over, Mr. Maverick."

"Have you now?"

"It's about that girl you escorted out to the shindig last night."

"Well, I sort of got the impression you weren't too interested in her?"

"Oh, I'm interested all right. I wish I wasn't, but Lord am I."

"How's that?"

"Well, you see, Mr. Maverick, before I left for Yale, I was, well, I was right soft on another girl. Cyndi-Jo Stroud, was her name."

"Oh?"

"Yes, and we sort of promised that we'd wait for each other. But last night, that angel with you, well, she sort of made me forget Cyndi-Jo."

"She did, huh?"

"For a while, anyway. And then I remembered and I felt real bad because it seemed like I wasn't being fair to Cyndi-Jo. So I went inside and I left the other girl to herself. I kept thinking about both girls and they sort of got mixed up in my mind. I couldn't even set them straight."

"Well now, that's quite the conundrum."

A lovely feminine voice interrupted us with a soft knock at the door.

"Yes. Excuse me."

"Good afternoon Mr. Maverick, it's Cyndi-Jo, may I come in?"

"Good afternoon, young lady."

"Mr. Maverick. I finally managed to get them…"

Tommy practically jumped out of his boots. "Cyndi-Jo!"

She feigned indifference. "Hello, Tommy."

His face held the innocence of a child picking wild flowers in a field. "Golly, it's good to see you! I was hoping you'd be at the dance last night."

Oh boy.

Her eyes narrowed "Were you now?"

Tommy was still obliviously puppy dog cheerful "You know, you haven't changed a bit!"

Son, you best clue in right fast...

Cyndi-Jo had steam coming out of her ears but focused on me instead. "No, I...reckon I...Uh...They're in this burlap bag, Mr. Maverick. I'm returning... Those things.... Yes, things I borrowed."

"Oh, right."

Her voice had a hollow ring to it. "I hoped maybe you could return them to Derek for me?"

I looked slowly at the both of them. "Well, I'm not sure just when I'll be running into him again, Cyndi-Jo."

She rolled her eyes, at a still clueless Tommy, then handed me the bag. "Here, Mr. Maverick. Now be careful... with this bag...Careful you don't ..."

"Oh, oh no Cyndi-Jo. I'm sorry, that there bag, just sort of slipped out of my fingers.... Well, here, I'll put these party slippers back in there now. There we go."

Tom's eyes went as wide as saucer plates in recognition. He looked at her, me, the slipper bag, then back at her, like a hog staring at a pocket watch.

I proclaimed, "I'm headed down for gumbo and pie. Goodbye and thanks for returning them. Goodbye, Tom."

Tom stared at her, then me, then back to Cyndi-Jo again.

Did he graduate from Yale?

"Cyndi-Jo, wait a minute!"

That's right boy!

She murmured, "What?"

"Where'd you get those shoes?"

Eureka!

Her tone was deceptively calm but she was getting red in the face. "Whatever do you mean?"

Then it finally hit him like a ton of bricks. "Why, they're the same ones that... They're exactly the same! Cyndi-Jo, why, you were at the square dance last night! You and that angel ...I mean...other girl. Why, there wasn't any other girl. It was you! No wonder I couldn't get you straightened out in my mind."

That did it.

She roared "What are you talking about?"

"Tell her, Mr. Maverick, what I told you just before she came in!"

"Well, I reckon maybe you'd best tell her yourself, Tom. As a matter of fact, I'm kind of anxious to get downstairs while there's still some pecan pie left."

I figured, *If that boy survives the next ten minutes, they'll live happily ever after.*

If.

As I made my way downstairs, there might as well have been a hurricane back behind me.

Now Tommy was fiery too, "So. Now you listen to me, Cyndi-Jo. I've been in love with you ever since I can remember!"

"I don't believe it!"

"Well, it's true. And it don't matter a lick what kind of a dress you wear or how your hair is fixed up!"

Well, there wasn't much point to my hanging around to see how Cyndi-Jo and Tom turned out.

It could have been a magic Nacogdoches night.

It could have been everything up to and including fairy tales are bigger in Texas.

Some things are just meant to be.

Of course you realize by now her married name would be, Mrs. Cyndi Ella.

There's only one way a Texas tale like this can end.

I reckon you know as well as I do...

They were just bound to live happily ever after.

BLIZZARD
AMARILLO TALE

"Don't go in if you don't know the way out."
— **New Mexico Proverb**

IT'S SOBERING TO REALIZE you need an early morning winter bath on the open range. The big Texas sky is so expansive that there are both true and untrue instances of just about everything described underneath it.

Take snow for instance.

Most folks would bet a pretty penny the Lone Star State is all desert, cactus and desperados.

They plumb wouldn't believe what I was staring at.

I'd never seen it myself in all my wanderings.

The Red River was frozen solid.

It was the coldest winter anyone could remember, and the old-timers were proven right that a Texas river could freeze if it got cold enough for long enough. I managed to break some ice into my hat and give Badger a drink. He gave me a look, wondering if his human was fool enough to skinny dip himself clean in an icy river.

I was.

Both Badger and I were covered in dust and I had a three-week beard. However, after a week or so of solitude, a break from beans and coffee and a night in a real bed was a mighty appealing notion. Amarillo was the closest town and it's one thing to be scruffy looking, but if you stink too, folks might take you for a saddle bum.

So, I got a fire going, coffee boiling and a blanket ready. Then I stripped down in that gray morning chill. I barely dipped in the river for an eternal second, and instantly realized I'd made an epic, teeth-chattering mistake. If it's possible for a horse to laugh and shake his head at silliness, I reckon Badger did just that.

Ice water will wake the dead.

However, the rejuvenative powers of a thick wool Mexican blanket, fresh clothes and lots of scalding black coffee set things right.

I'd spent the winter haying cattle up at the Sangre de Cristo. That's God's country up there. A storm had been brewing as I left New Mexico, and it sure seemed to follow me mighty personal like.

One look at the red sky that morning told me a blizzard was stewing here as well. We got going just as the winds flared up and it began snowing. It was about a three-hour ride to Amarillo.

Then it started hailing something fierce.

The midwinter sun deserted the dark hazel sky. The wind drilled down into us and the air was as thin as I could ever recall. A look to the sky behind me to the east revealed a great slab of swirling blackness descending upon the plain. That black slab of blizzard would be right down on top of me before I reached town.

This was the kind of weather that kills the land and everything on it.

I needed to find shelter fast.

A high wind will distemper a man and dull his senses like he's drunk. It might have been thirty minutes later the black sky gave way to whiteout. I couldn't see or hear much of anything anymore over the shrilling wind, and I smelled moisture in the air like I was underwater.

The blizzard howled around us. I couldn't look left or right without hail stinging my face blind like small birdshot. I only knew if I kept the wind on my back I was headed west toward town.

The icy squall was pounding us, and I could feel Badger slowing down and weakening under me. My body stiffened with icy shards in my beard, and I started feeling drowsy. Men died easy when caught out in the elements like this.

Badger was one fine horse and giving me all he had, but now his head was down close to the ground. I figured he'd stumble down before long and kicked my feet out of the stirrups and braced myself against the saddle horn.

The wind had truly near sapped the strength out of me when I smelled smoke from a blur to the south. I turned Badger toward the smell, hoping beyond hope.

Then, I saw the blur of a small cabin up ahead.

I thought for sure my mind was playing tricks on me.

The wooden door was icy but it was real.

I slid down off Badger, with a frozen smile, and pounded on the door. The door finally creaked open and a shadowy figure stood in the light.

"Who are you?"

"Bring him in, Silas! Any man out in that weather is good and harmless."

"All right you, get inside!"

"Out of the way, Silas, you fool! Stranger, get them hands in the air high!"

My vision was still a bit groggy, but there were two of them and they had me covered with a shotgun. The wild-eyed one called Silas was a pasty, reed-thin little man who clearly carried his brains in his back pocket.

The other fellow was paunchy, grizzled and graying. His ice-blue eyes were crow-tracked at the corners and they pierced a man like an ice pick.

The little one took my pistol and the older one pointed to the stove.

"You can sit up to this stove now, but don't try nothing or I'll cut you in half with buckshot."

Silas said, "Look Harlan, this is a mighty fancy pistol."

The older one, Harlan, sat on the stool by the stove, a shotgun across his knees, and those cold eyes never left me. "You look half-froze, stranger. You must have wanted something powerful bad to be out in a blizzard this bad."

Silas squinted. "I never saw him around here before, Harlan. He's a stranger, maybe he was just looking for some cows and got lost in the storm?"

Harlan grumbled, "Sometimes I'm amazed you know enough to spit downwind, Silas. You just don't know much...Stella! Hey, Stella, get on out here!"

She was a pretty girl, but bruised up with a dark, half-wild look that I'd never seen before in a woman. Her eyes jumped from Silas to Harlan and then came to rest on me, fixed, pleading and curious. Then, after a moment she looked down and away and moved into a chair across the room.

Her voice was a hoarse whisper: "Supper's ready."

Harlan said, "Stella, it's awful cold out, you recognize him? You ever seen him before now?"

She shook her head.

"You're sure now, maybe Amarillo, maybe you saw him up there sometime?"

"I don't know him."

"You're sure?"

Stella nodded emphatically

Harlan's eyes went dark. "If you're lying to me, you know what I'll do to you later—it'll truly hurt you bad this time around."

"Honest, I never saw him before!"

Silas said, "He come in here half dead right out of the ice blizzard. Maybe he just got lost?"

Harlan snapped, "Hobble your lips, Silas! We don't know what he's doing here!"

My body had finally warmed to the point I trusted my voice. "Why shouldn't a man get out of the storm like this?"

Harlan cocked the scattergun and pointed at me. "That's enough out of you, stranger. We never saw you before, we don't know who you are and as soon as I think you're lying I'm going to blow a big hole in you."

"What about my horse? I'd like to put him in the barn if you've got one."

"Silas, get his horse in the barn."

The little man shook his head, "No chance, I ain't going outside to freeze."

"That horse will freeze if you don't and we might need it. Go on, Silas, before I get good and vexed."

Silas gave me an ugly glare then trudged outside.

Stella repeated, "Supper's ready."

Harlan grunted, "Leave it be. I want to talk to our friend here first—maybe we won't have to feed him."

Stella whispered, "The meat will get cold."

Harlan glared at her then fixed his eyes on me, "Who cares, I'm mighty curious about you, mister."

"So it seems."

Those old evil eyes gleamed, "Don't you poke fun at me. Get me mad, mister, and this here shotgun will blow your guts all over the wall!"

"The meat will be boiled soggy if we don't eat soon," Stella mumbled.

Harlan backhanded her across the face in response. Tears swelled up in her eyes as a trickle of blood dripped from a cut on her lip.

"You just don't listen no other way, do you, Stella? Sometimes I think you just like it rough."

Silas leered at her like a lusty weasel, "Yeah, she likes everything rough."

I asked, "What is it you want to know about me?"

Harlan looked at Stella, then me, and cracked a wicked toothy smile.

"I can tell how to handle you easy now, mister."

"How's that?"

"I reckon all I got to do is smack the girl and you'll talk. I don't have to do nothing to you."

"Can I take my jacket off? I've warmed up now."

"Wait, you might have a Derringer hidden up in there."

"He can raise his hands, I'll unbutton it." Stella said.

Harlan muttered, "Well now that's right smart of you, Stella. Be quick about it."

Her hands brushed an old bill of sale in my coat pocket.

She didn't let on.

Harlan didn't miss a thing.

"Stella, come over here. Drop his jacket and hold out your other hand. Open it now!"

He kept me covered with the shotgun and took the folded paper from her hand.

"Stella, Stella, Stella." He shook his head. "Don't you ever learn? That's bad what you just done. Now, you know what I got to do. After you've cleaned up supper I'll put you outside in that blizzard for a spell. You think good on that until then."

He read the signature on the paper. "Wade Maverick? You're really him, mister?"

I nodded.

"Well, Mr. Red Gun, you shouldn't have come here."

"I was lucky to find this place in the storm."

Silas slammed open the door, ushering in a bone-chilling wind gust, and banged it shut behind him. His coat was caked in ice and he stomped his feet for warmth.

Harlan asked, "There wasn't sign of nobody outside, Silas?"

"What? Why"

"Because, Silas, somebody might have come along, a friend of Maverick here."

Silas asked, "Maverick, who's that?"

"I'm Wade Maverick."

"Silas, did you see other horse tracks or anything?"

"No tracks at all." Silas cocked his head sideways. "Harlan, I knows that name. That's the fellow they call the Red Gun. He must be after us!"

I asked, "Would I have walked in here like I did if I was on a posse?"

Harlan stated, "Maybe the frost muddled your head. Where'd you ride from, Maverick, and where were you headed?"

"New Mexico and Amarillo. What are you and Silas on the run for?"

"Don't you tell him squat, Harlan. I don't trust him one bit!"

Harlan laughed, "Silas, it would be mighty dull without you, boy."

Silas snapped, "Don't nobody laugh at me, Harlan! Stop it!"

"Hush, Silas. It don't matter what Maverick knows. He ain't ever leaving this place. We'll kill him and bury him somewhere."

"Right. Why didn't I think of that?"

"Because I do the thinking for us, Silas, that's why. What was it exactly you'd like to know, Maverick?"

"Stop your games, Harlan."

"Me and Silas are wanted for murder over in Oklahoma City. It's a mite unfair though, as we didn't aim to kill nobody. We was just robbing a bank and a couple of the people there wouldn't do what we told them. Silas cut one good, and we had to shoot our way out. You know how it goes."

"Yeah."

Silas added, "It ain't hardly fair we're wanted for murder and we didn't even get so much money!"

"I see. What about Stella, and whose place is this anyway?"

She answered like a mouse. "It's my place now that Pa's gone."

I asked, "You mean you were living in a cabin out here all alone?"

"No."

"They killed your pa, is that it?"

"Yes."

"How long ago?"

"I can't recall, maybe a month."

Silas grinned. "It's been thirty-six days."

"Silas is good with numbers." Harlan cackled.

"What you do with him?"

Silas said, "Who, her pa? Oh, we buried the old man out back in the pasture."

Harlan added with mock indignation, "We couldn't quite afford a fancy funeral, could we, Silas? Of course we took right proper care of Stella. We made a woman out of her!"

"All right Harlan, now that we done told him everything, let's shoot him."

"No, I've been thinking it over. Folks in Amarillo are likely expecting Maverick here. If he don't show up after a spell, they might come looking for him."

"But Harlan, earlier you said we can just bury him, right?"

"Yeah, but we can't bury his horse in this frozen soil. Even if we set the horse loose and they find it, but not him, then they'll still figure something's up."

"You got it all planned out, I see."

"Let's just kill him now, Harlan—I'm getting hungry."

Stella said, "That supper won't be fit to eat."

Silas snapped, "Shut your trap, Stella, or I'll cut you again! Let's end him, Harlan, I'm right hungry."

Harlan replied, "No, listen up. We'll knock Maverick over the head and toss him outside to freeze. He'll keep real good in this cold. After the blizzard breaks, we can take him out ten miles and dump him on the ground. It'll look like he got throwed, hit his head, and froze!"

Silas smirked, "That's a mighty fine plan, Harlan."

"Yeah, then we'll break his horse's leg to make it easier for them to find him."

"The horse?" I asked. "You just don't care about anything, do you, Harlan?"

He grinned. "I care about me, and sometimes Silas."

Silas nodded. "Sure, me and Harlan are friends, ain't we, Harlan."

"Of course we need the snow to melt, since we can't leave tracks for them to follow back there."

Silas repeated, "Harlan, we're still gonna kill him now, right?'

"We sure are."

Harlan ordered, "You keep him covered and I'll get up behind and bash him. I'll hit him with that branding iron by the fire."

I said, "Harlan, there's no limit to how low you slither, is there?"

"How's that?"

"You'd leave a man unfed before killing him?"

Silas was back and ready with the poker.

Harlan gave me a long look. "Leave it be, Silas, we'll all eat first."

It wasn't four in the afternoon, but the blizzard had darkened the land and its blackness blanketed the windows. Along the warped wooden walls of the cabin, tiny rivulets of snow trickled through to the floor.

Harlan sat directly behind me in the kitchen while I ate, then changed places with Silas to eat himself. His mind seemed a dark cavern to me. He was a vicious brute with no conscience and the predatory instincts of a reptile that killed whatever got close enough to be struck. Every living creature was his enemy. As for Silas, well other than the fact he savored cutting people and was crazy as a bullbat, there was no way to explain him. There was just something wrong with that cretin.

Stella was my only chance. Harlan had pretty much beaten the tar out of her to break her spirit. Supper was over soon enough, but Harlan seemed in no particular rush to follow through with his plans.

She still talks back so they haven't broken her yet.

Harlan ordered, "Keep your trap shut and clean up these tin plates, Stella. You can cluck your head off when you're outside alone. I'll learn you to obey me if I have to break your neck."

Silas sounded concerned. "Now don't do that yet, Harlan. At least until we're ready to pull out anyways."

"Why not?"

"Well, I ain't fixing to do the cooking."

"No, I've eaten your cooking. All right Silas, give me the shotgun. Maverick, get back by the stove while Stella clears this mess."

"Should we crack his skull now and throw him out to freeze?"

"Not just yet. Stella's punishment comes first."

"Harlan, you know, someday you're gonna get caught without that shotgun. A man like me would tear you apart."

He chuckled. "Fair enough, Maverick."

"Give me a fair chance at you then."

Harlan gave me the side eye, "What?"

"Fight me barehanded, if you're man enough?"

"No dice, Maverick."

Silas pouted. "It's time, Harlan, I want to get to bed soon."

"Stella, now you get outside like I told you. Girl you best git, and don't open that door so wide or you'll blow the lamp out!"

Stella walked across the room and out the front door without a glance at any of us.

She'll head out to the barn and be fine for a bit.

I got to make my move soon.

I sure wasn't gonna sit there like a Christmas goose and let Silas knock my head open when he got in place. It made even less sense to try to jump Harlan with both barrels of that scattergun shotgun pointed right at my chest.

I'd gotten myself caught between a rock and a hard place, and the more I thought about it the madder I got.

Silas whined, "Harlan, I'm tuckered out. I'm gonna hit him and go to bed. You can do what you want after, but I ain't staying up all night."

Harlan smiled, "Silas's got his mind made up. Adios, Maverick."

I snickered, "Just what do you call a mind like that, Harlan?"

Silas sneered, "I got ways to fix you, Maverick!"

"Hold up, Silas! We best wrap something around that branding iron, otherwise it won't look like he hit his head on a rock."

"What difference does it make?"

"Just do as I say, Silas!"

Silas rolled his eyes, "Fine, Harlan. I'll use this curtain here."

Harlan ordered, "Keep your eyes on me, Maverick."

Silas moved around behind me and was getting a good grip on the iron.

I tensed slightly forward in the chair, waiting for the split second when instinct told me to jump.

Suddenly, the door blasted wide open as a powerful gust of freezing nocturnal wind roared through the cabin.

The lamp flared out instantly and I threw myself sideways out of the chair just as the shotgun blasted over me.

Harlan roared. "Did you bash him, Silas? Did you get him, you bloody fool? Maverick, don't you try nothing. I got some more shells right here. Don't you move boy, hear me!"

I crawled across the room and was out the icy door into the darkness before Harlan could reload. I got to my feet in the thick snow outside. I turned back to see Stella waiting by the side of the door with a pitchfork in her hand.

She was shaking with cold and leaning up against the wall. I could hear Harlan fumbling around the cabin. I reached out and took the pitchfork from her, flattened myself against the wall, and waited.

She whispered in the howling wind, "I was afraid it was you he shot."

"Great trick, Stella—throwing the door open that way saved me."

"He shot Silas, didn't he?"

"Yeah, point blank with buckshot."

I put my finger on my nose for silence.

Harlan roared. "Maverick, I'm going to kill you and the girl good and painful like!"

It wasn't clear Harlan would come out the door before my hands were too frozen to hold the pitchfork.

It seemed we waited an eternity in that frigid howling nocturnal wind.

The barrel of the shotgun finally appeared waist high from the doorway. It began to focus its way around toward our direction. This was foolhardy on his part, but a man behind a gun often gets a false sense of security and power.

Once the barrel extended about four inches past the icy doorframe, I slammed the pitchfork down on it with all my might. The shotgun clattered harmlessly to the ground as he fell forward to a knee in the doorway. I stabbed the pitchfork up into his chest as he tried to stand, knocking him back off his feet and pinning him bug-eyed to the cabin floor. He wheezed and went limp with a prong straight through the heart.

Then I scooped up the shotgun.

"Did you get him?"

"Yeah."

"He's dead?"

"Yes, get inside and light the lantern."

"My fingers are too stiff."

"Let me do it."

The lamp illuminated a gory mess from hell. Silas's face was blown away and Harlan's death mask was hateful to the end.

"Oh my god."

"I'll clean this up, go wait by the stove."

"I'm all right, Mr. Maverick, but I can't help you much till I warm up some."

"Get over to the stove. I'll drag these bodies outside...And Stella."

"Yes?"

"I think you can call me Wade at this point."

She almost smiled. "Thank you."

ՍՍՍՍՍՍՍՍ

I woke up the next morning wondering if this had all been a nightmare.

The smell of fresh-brewed coffee confirmed I was alive.

"Come on out to the kitchen Wade, it's warm there and I got some hot coffee for you."

"That sounds bully to me."

Stella said, "It looks like the storm's lifted, but it's mighty cold out."

"The cold is one thing, but that wind is a killer."

"Here, get some of this coffee in you."

"Stella, this is a mighty fine cup of coffee."

"Tell me something, Wade."

"What's that?"

"You will tell me the truth now?"

"Yes."

"Promise?"

"Sure, about what?"

"Are you married?"

"I'd make a poor husband for any woman, Stella."

"Thank you, Wade, thanks for putting it nice like that."

"Stella, I reckon it's time to leave this place."

She nodded, "I'll never come back here myself."

I asked, "Where will you go?"

"I got three good horses. I'll ride up to Amarillo, sell them, then buy some pretty dresses. I'll find a place. It won't be hard, not after this."

"I wish I could help you."

"You have, but I can take care of myself."

"Stella,...I, uh...Look, all men aren't like them."

She looked through my soul with old dead eyes.

I didn't know what to say.

"Hey, I'll at least stop at the nearest ranch and tell the men to come here and take care of these bodies."

She shook her head, "Don't bother, I'm burning this place to Hell as soon as you leave."

"Well, goodbye, Stella."

"Goodbye Wade, look me up in Amarillo if you ever pass through."

"I will."

A few minutes later I'd saddled Badger up and was on the trail to Dallas. The sky hung slate gray and low across the horizon as far as the eye could see.

No killer wind, though.

The prairie was still white, bitter and frigid.

There wasn't a sign of life to be found.

It was like the feeling I got the time I was forced to cut across ancient Indian burial grounds. It was a ghostly, hollow feeling. I felt like a trespasser, as though something had gone wrong. Then I realized what the past few days had been.

Facing pure evil.

Badger and I were at the Red River once more. It was still cold and icy, but that salty southern river was running again. The sun cut its way through the haunting clouds, reflecting its warming rays across the ripples of the river.

A high-pitched cry emanated from above with the fluttering of powerful wings. A magnificent bald eagle had flown down through the fresh sunlight and plucked a glistening trout from the waters. It settled down in the icy branches of a frozen oak tree on the opposite bank.

The eagle began eating the fish, then paused to stare at Badger and me with those pale yellow eyes. I was savoring the sunshine while rubbing down Badger's neck and giving him a drink from my hat.

The eagle finished the fish, gave us a parting look, and soared back up into the heavens.

Damn straight.

Life goes on.

Ingrid Ekberg

Houston Tale

THE CHINABERRY TREES IN these parts tend to lean northeastward on account of the prevailing southwestern winds. It wasn't just immigrants who'd come to Texas—they'd brought in trees and such as well. In some cases these unions bore fruit, in others not so much. You either adapted to Texas or she broke you.

It was Friday morning when I got to Houston and my first trip to town in over a month. I'd signed on for branding season at the Briscoe Ranch. Old man Briscoe needed to raise money for feed, so he asked me to drive about a dozen of his steers in and sell them at Saturday's auction.

I turned the cattle over to the auctioneer, Greg Prince, and it took a few hours to get them all sorted out. By noon, I was good and hungry and wandered over to Christie's Café.

Christie's food was real good too, fresh biscuits with gobs of butter, honey-fried chicken and mashed potatoes with creamy gravy. Dessert was truly the thing to holler about though. They had the best cinnamon apple pie outside of German Hill Country.

There was only one drawback to eating there: Pat Christie.

I liked Pat, but he could speak ten words a second with gusts to fifty.

Lordy, but the man could cook.

I just sat there nodding and contemplating a second helping of pie, wondering if Pat's tongue ever rested.

"Are you listening, Wade? Also Burke Koonce, he's a marshal now, but I reckon you knew that, didn't you?"

"As a matter of fact I didn't."

"Of course, surely, he was elected last August. There was over a hundred votes cast in the election. That's the biggest election Houston's ever had. Imagine that! Heck, it might even be the biggest election in this part of Texas for all I know."

I grunted thanks as he scooped a second piece of pie onto my plate.

"Thanks, Well, yes that is something."

"Well, unless you count Austin, over there they ain't very particular who they let vote or run for office...Why I hear tell there was a Yankee carpetbagger passing through the town last election day, and they just drug him right off to the polls."

"You don't say?"

He refilled my coffee cup without missing a beat.

Great coffee too.

"Yes sir, let me tell you if there was to be an honest census, we'd show up with a good hundred more people in Houston. I tell you, them Austin government types can't be trusted…Why I…"

"Well, this sure was one mighty fine meal, Pat."

"Now just where do you reckon you're headed off to, Wade?"

Three choices for peace and quiet. Shoot myself, shoot Pat, or help myself to a third piece of pie.

Pat didn't even blink and scooped more pie onto my plate.

Pie it is. I'd surely hang for shooting the best cook in East Texas.

"Heck, Wade, you ain't even let me tell you about Marshal Koonce finding Gus Patterson's body!"

"Huh?"

"Just what did you think I was leading up to?"

"I don't know. Tell me."

"It was a week ago, last Monday, that's when it happened."

"I see."

"The reason I remember so plain is, just about eleven o'clock in the morning it started to thunder something powerful. I saw Mrs. Fletcher running down Main Street holding a copy of the *Houston Post* over her head. Of course, she shouldn't be fooled by a little bit of thunder. Everyone knows it don't rain until September in these parts... I lived in Houston for twenty years and it mostly never rains in August.... No, sir!"

"What about Mr. Patterson?"

"Well I was just coming to that, Wade, can't you give a body a minute?"

"Oh right, sure Pat."

"Now where was I?"

"Last Monday?"

"Oh yes. Old Gus's body was lying on the floor of his parlor when Marshal Koonce come in. I heard the place looked like he put up quite a fight too. They say there was broken furniture and glass all over the place."

"How did he die?"

"A slug in his chest, that's what killed him. The shooting must have been around ten o'clock that morning...That's right. At least that's when Mrs. Oakley said she heard what sounded like a shot. You know the Oakleys, Wade? They're the neighbors, just a down the road

a bit from Gus Patterson's ranch."

"Yup, sure. I know them."

"Clint Oakley, he's that short towheaded fellow who married Betty Wilkinson."

"I said I knew him, Pat."

"Now there's no need to take my head off. I'm just trying to give you all the facts!"

"Sorry, you go right ahead and tell me the facts."

"Well, let's see, where was I? Well that's the trouble. A fellow interrupts you and you lose your entire train of thought...Oh yeah, Gus Patterson. I reckon that's all there is to tell. The trial was last Wednesday."

"A trial already?"

"Yes sir, Rod Hedlund is the fellow that killed Gus."

"Rod Hedlund?"

"What's gotten with you, Wade? Ain't you listening to me?"

I reckon my face went as dark as a pocket.

"Huh? Well, you know you kind of neglected to mention Rod Hedlund before Pat."

"I did?"

"Yeah."

'Oh sorry, well there weren't no doubt but that he was the guilty party. Hedlund still had the $400 in his pocket when Marshal Koonce arrested him."

"$400?"

"That how much money he stole from Gus."

"I see."

"You know, Rod Hedlund never struck me as the type to...Well, I guess you just never can tell about people, can you?"

"Oh, I didn't realize you was a friend of Rod's, Wade."

"Well, I wouldn't go so far as to call us friends. We did a cattle drive to Abilene once. He always seemed like a decent young fellow. His pa, was a true bronc buster back in the day. We rode for the same brand when I was but a pilgrim."

"Yeah, well Rod admitted to robbing Gus. Except he says that when he come in Gus was already dead, and the strongbox was just sitting right there all nice and open like. He sure must think we're a bunch of country bumpkins expecting anyone to believe a yarn like that."

"I reckon it's possible what he says might be true."

"A local jury of his peers ruled otherwise. The hanging is scheduled for Monday."

"The hanging's on Monday?"

"We got law and order in Houston."

"Yeah, I reckon I owe you two bits, huh?"

"Let me fetch your change...Now I'll be doggone...She's still there.... Why is that girl still over in front of the depot? She come in on the morning express from Dallas...The poor soul's been standing there since near nine o'clock."

I glanced out the back window.

A blind man would have seen her.

She was young and shapely in a red dress. Her back was to us and her long chestnut-brown hair was swirling in the breeze. She was fidgety, tapping a foot on the ground, and shaking her head like a woman only does when she's good and annoyed with a man.

"I reckon she's waiting for somebody to meet her."

"That's funny, I ain't heard of nobody expecting visitors. I usually get wind of that sort of thing."

"Yeah, Pat, I imagine you do."

"Here's your change, Wade, good to jaw with you again."

"Yeah, I'll be seeing you, Pat."

"You're going to be in town for a spell, ain't you?"

"No, I'm heading back to Briscoe Ranch tomorrow morning."

"That's a shame. You'll miss the hanging."

"I reckon as much. So long."

ᴗᴗᴗᴗᴗᴗᴗ

The girl waiting on the station platform spun around as I passed by.

It took my breath away.

She was as lovely a girl as I'd ever seen.

Her deep crystal-blue eyes were mesmerizing, and she couldn't have been a day over twenty. Men don't know so much about dresses, but I don't recall seeing one like it in Texas before. It was right pretty with a little bow and a flower pattern on it.

She seems German or the like.

Whoever she's waiting on is one lucky fellow.

It sure looked like she intended to stay around Houston for a spell. She had two great big canvas suitcases and an overflowing wicker basket with her.

I smiled and tipped my hat to her.

She was frowning, kind of anxious like, and clearly irritated. She studied me as if she was trying to make up her mind about something.

"Excuse me for bothering you, miss, but is there anything I can do for you?"

"You come to meet me, mister?"

She had a nice voice and a heavy foreign accent.

"Oh, uh no, no."

"Ja, I see now. You are not him."

"How's that?"

"He's a different looking man. Shorter than you. I remember from pictures."

"Then you were waiting on somebody?"

"Oh ja, for sure."

"Well, maybe if you told me who it is, I'd be able to find him for you."

"It is man I came to marry."

"Oh, oh I see."

"We write letters over two years now. He have family in same part of Sweden where I live. I am Swedish, mister."

"Yes, yes, I sort of figured as much."

"Then he send me money to come to America. I think he must be a rich fellow. He send me two hundred dollars, so much money."

"Hmm, yes, that's a good amount of money all right."

"He tell me stay with my sister in Wisconsin till he make some more. I stay there three months, then I get tired waiting. I still have forty dollar left so I take train west."

"Right, well maybe he didn't know you were getting in today."

"No, we write him letter from Wisconsin. My sister help me. I not so at language English good."

My god this girl's got grit. She came alone all the way from Europe to marry a fellow she's never met.

"No, no, you're talking just fine. He must be busy working or the like. But he will come."

"I do not worry."

"Well, that's good."

"Mister?"

"Yes?"

"Are you his friend, maybe?"

"Well, I don't know. You didn't tell me his name."

"Oh." She laughed heartily. "I very foolish girl sometimes. I need to use my brains. It is Rod."

"Rod?"

"Yes, Rod Hedlund."

I managed to keep a straight face.

"You know him?"

"Yes, yes, I do."

"You no see Rod anywhere today?"

"No, no, I haven't seen him."

"Please forgive my manners, I never ask your name or tell my name either."

"It's Maverick, Wade Maverick."

"I am Ingrid Ekberg. You are a nice man, Mr. Maverick."

"Oh, it's a pleasure, Miss Ekberg."

"Why you look at me like that, mister?"

"Well..."

"Something is bad?"

"Yeah, yeah, I'm afraid so."

"Oh no, Rod, he is not sick?"

"No, not sick...You see, Miss Ekberg..."

"Just tell, please."

"You said you came to Texas to marry Rod?"

"Ja, I do."

"But you don't really know him, do you?"

"We write so many letters, me and Rod."

"Yes, but just letters, right?"

Her brow furled in annoyance. "You think I cannot love a man I never meet?"

"I didn't say that."

"I know Rod say this many letters as if we meet a hundred times. We tell each other everything in letters."

"Maybe so, maybe so, but I..."

Her eyes narrowed and her face flushed crimson.

"I see, Mr. Maverick. You are his friend. I see what it is you think."

"No, it's just…"

"You think I only marry Rod because he send me so much money!"

"No, no, no, of course not."

"I am good girl, Mr. Maverick! I marry Rob because I love him. I never see him, but I love him. This only reason!"

"I believe you, Miss Ekberg…. Look, maybe let's get you out of this glaring sun and talk over coffee at the café?"

"No, thank you, but I must be here when Rod comes."

"Well, I'm afraid Rod isn't coming."

"I do not understand."

"I'm awful sorry to tell you about this, but Rod's in jail."

"Jail?"

"Yes."

"You mean police arrest him?"

"Marshal Koonce did."

"What did Rod do? Let me think, maybe he scared to meet me and drink too much?"

"No, it's serious."

"Tell me, Mr. Maverick."

"Folks say that he killed a man last week."

"Rod killed a man?"

"It sure seems that way."

"No, it could not be. Rod is fine good feller."

"Yes, well I reckon I was surprised as well".

"They make mistake, I tell them big mistake. Then, they let my Rod go...Where is jail?"

"No, that's a bad idea."

"Please, where is jail? Is that it there?"

"Yes, but..."

"Thank you very much."

She cradled her wicker basket to her body, grabbed both suitcases, and began stumbling toward the jail.

"Hey now, let me give you a hand with those things."

"No help please. I am strong girl."

"Now Miss Ekberg, I'm afraid the marshal will..."

"Goodbye Mr. Maverick, you come to wedding, ja?"

"I, uh, good luck."

UUUUUUUU

Well, it certainly wasn't my place to tell her about the hanging on Monday. She'd find out soon enough.

Life's surely harsh sometimes.

I strolled around town for an hour or so and then got myself a room at the Buffalo Bayou Hotel. There was an old copy of the *Houston Post* on the desk table. The main article was about the Patterson shoot and Rod Hedlund's trial.

I skimmed through it for a couple of minutes.

A knock at the door was the hotel clerk. He told me a foreign lady was asking for me in the lobby.

"Hello, Miss Ekberg?"

"They tell me I find you here…We must talk, it's important."

"Well, won't you sit down?"

"I would rather stand, I am too nervous for sit down. Mr. Maverick."

"Yes?"

What is wrong with Marshal Burke? Is he bad man?"

"No, he's not."

"He said Rod must be hanged."

"Yeah."

"Well, that is not possible. They would not hang a man who is not guilty."

"Well, Miss Ekberg, maybe Rod is guilty."

"No! He is not. The marshal let me talk to Rod. I asked him if he does this awful thing…

He tells me no!"

"Well,…I don't know what to say."

"Rod no lie. A woman knows when her man lies. Rod is fine fellow. Better even than I hope. My sister warned me I should not expect too much. So I not disappointed. But Rod, he is good, kind and handsome. No doubt in my mind, he could not be the one to kill any man."

"Well, he has admitted to stealing Gus Patterson's money."

"He did it for me. That is why he takes it, so we can get married…I know is very wrong to steal and he must be punished for it."

"Well, if he was willing to steal…"

"The steal is not to kill."

"They hang for killing, yes?"

"Usually."

"I tell Rod that we meet. That you are very nice to me."

"Oh."

"He says you be a famous person with the funny name…The Red Gun."

"I see."

"Then you must stop them. Rod says you can prove he is not guilty. Will you talk to marshal for him?"

"Well, I don't see what me talking to Marshal Koonce would do."

"Please, Mr. Maverick…I tell you something now. Before I say I come to marry Rod because I am in love with him because of letters. More truth is I always wanted to come to America. I think this my only chance, but after I meet him and talk, I know I love Rod and they will kill him in three days. Rod is innocent, Mr. Maverick…. You must believe me!"

"All right, I'll talk to him."

I left Ingrid at the hotel and I went over to see Marshal Koonce. The office was in the front part of the jail where they were keeping Rod Hedlund. He hadn't been a marshal long but had had several years' deputy experience. He knew the job and seemed the even-keeled type that usually made a good marshal.

He was polite and humble.

"I sure felt terrible, Mr. Maverick, when Miss Ekberg came in here and told me who she was and what she wanted. I let her talk to Hedlund, figured it was the least I could do."

"That was good of you."

"No, it just seemed to make things worse. He convinced her that he was innocent and I was out to get him."

"Well, nobody's going to believe that."

"That there girl might believe it. Love's blind. I guess, I wouldn't blame her if she did. Hedlund's a pretty smooth talker at that."

"Yeah.... Hey, there couldn't be any doubt about it, could there?"

"How so?"

"I mean, as I understand it, Rod says that Patterson was already dead when he got there."

"He sure did."

"He said he took the money because, well, it was just too tempting."

"It don't stand to reason that somebody'd murder Gus and then go off without breaking into a strongbox. Now, does it, Wade?"

"No, I guess it doesn't."

"Besides, Mrs. Oakley seen Rod riding away from the ranch not five minutes after she heard a shot."

"Right. Did you arrest him the same day?"

"Well, I came into town right after I found Gus's body.

"Mrs. Oakley had sent for me. She had a feeling something was wrong

"Hedlund keeps a small room at Widow McGregor's rooming house just off Main Street. That's where I found him."

"Did he still have the gun on him?"

"No, he claimed he didn't own a .45 which is what the slug in Gus's chest was. A search of his room didn't turn up a thing."

"I see."

"Now, Rod had plenty of time to get rid of the gun. Look, there's no limit to the number of places between Gus's ranch and town where he could have ditched it."

"That's true enough. Does anybody ever remember seeing Rod with a .45?"

"Not that I know of. Wait a minute. Mr. Maverick, you ain't taking Rod's side in this mess, are you?"

"No, I don't have a side. I'm just asking some questions."

"This was a cold-blooded killing. If you go out to Gus's place, you'll see. The poor old fellow sure put up a darn good fight for his life."

"Marshal, do you mind if I take you up on that invitation about seeing Gus's place?"

He shook his head then produced a key. "I need your word you won't touch nothing and come right back."

"I promise."

He handed over the key.

UUUUUUU

It was getting on toward dusk when I reached Gus Patterson's ranch house.

Gus had lived alone.

They hadn't straightened things up since the murders. Marshal Koonce was right, there sure had been a whale of a fight in the parlor. There were several broken chairs, bloodstains across the furniture and glass from a lamp that had been shattered against the fireplace.

The strongbox was gone too. They likely took it for the evidence.

I poked around for about half an hour, then headed back to town. A full-on Comanche Moon popped up about half an hour after sunset. It made the night bright enough to raid by, though there was little risk of that since the treaty.

That bright orange moon still had an eerie effect. Trusty Badger was normally as sure-footed as cat. Except he got downright skittish when a big old black bat winged just overhead. It was chirping up a storm and had come from a dense grove of salt cedars.

My horse was good and spooked and I was half flying off the saddle before he settled down. I was looking off the road toward the grove for more bats when I saw it.

A piece of metal glinting by amber moonlight. It was sticking out from a pile of dark leaves at the base of some thornbushes. It could have been any number of things.

But, even before I pulled it out from underneath the leaves and the dirt, I knew it was a gun.

The following morning, Miss Ekberg came into Christie's Café while I was finishing my coffee.

"Good morning, Mr. Maverick, did you talk with Marshal Koonce?"

"Yeah, I sure did."

"Did you tell him Rod did not kill this man? Rod is innocent."

"No, Miss Ekberg, I couldn't tell him that."

"Why?"

"Rod's guilty. I found his gun, the gun he used to kill Gus Patterson."

"No!"

"It was hidden in a gully about a few miles from the ranch house."

"I do not believe you!"

"I gave it to Marshal Burke. Rod's initials are right on the handle. Only one bullet had been fired. It's the right gun. There's no doubt now. If you want to see it for yourself, go over there."

"No, no, it could not be!"

"Now, Miss Ekberg, now listen to me. I'm telling you this because after Monday there won't be anything you can do about Rod. It'll be best you just forget him."

"I will not forget him, ever!"

"I know this isn't easy. You came all the way from Sweden, it's rough, but maybe it's best you found out before it was too late."

"Why, must you lie to me too, Mr. Maverick?"

"This is the truth, I'm sorry."

"You say you will show Rod's gun, what does he say?".

"He denies it."

"Then I deny it, too!"

"I'm sorry, Miss Ekberg, I guess there's nothing more I can do about it."

She erupted like a smoking hornet's nest.

"You lie to me, you and marshal.... Our love is not criminal! I do not understand.

In old country they say America is the best country in the world. This is a lie too! Where is justice? Where is freedom? They hang a man for what he does not do!"

"Now, Miss Ekberg, listen to me..."

"It's a horrible, terrible country...I wish I never come here.... I have no friend, no husband. I'm alone in country I hate!"

"I'm sorry. And, if there's any way I can help you. If you need some money to take the train back to your sisters, I can loan it to..."

"I want no help from Americans!"

She stormed out of the café like a heartbroken angel with clipped wings.

Then she reappeared momentarily in the doorway with tears flowing. "Mr. Maverick…I…God bless you…You are wrong, but good man in bad country."

There was only one possible thing left to do.

I'd lost my appetite and wandered over to the jail. I asked Marshal Koonce if I could talk to Rod some more.

He was skeptical but agreed.

To be honest, I didn't think it would do much good either.

Rod was about twenty-five or so. He was tall and towheaded with weathered skin, green eyes and a rugged build.

"To what do I owe the pleasure, Wade?"

"I thought maybe by now you'd feel like coming out with the truth."

"I told you the truth before. I've never seen that gun in my whole life. I ain't the only man with those initials, am I? Besides, what's the difference? I'm gonna hang Monday anyway."

"The difference is Miss Ekberg."

"Ingrid?"

"She loves you and believes in you, Rod. She believes you're innocent. And as long as you go on saying so, she's gonna keep on believing it…Even… Even after Monday."

"It's kind of nice to have somebody believe in me, Wade. Nobody else ever did."

"Now, that's a load of bull, I know your father for one! Rod, you weren't railroaded. You killed a man and had a fair trial, but Miss Ekberg doesn't realize that. She's young, she's upset, and she's in a strange country. All her dreams have turned sour."

"Maybe it's a good thing she woke up, Texas is a hell on earth!"

"We'll never agree on that. I think this is a pretty good place to live. But Miss Ekberg won't find that out, not if she goes on feeling this way."

"So you want that I confess to murdering Gus Patterson just so Ingrid can appreciate America?"

"It's more than that and you know it."

"If you ask me, this country ain't so hot anyway."

"A lot of good folks would argue tooth and nail against that."

"You're just wasting your breath."

"Yeah, I guess I am...I've known you, and your pa, since you were just a button. I never thought you'd grow into the type who'd kill Gus Patterson in cold blood the way you did."

"It wasn't cold blood. I didn't even...All right, but I ain't telling you this because of...

"I don't even know why I'm telling you. I needed money for Ingrid so we could get married. I wanted to make good the promises in the letters I wrote her. Everyone said old Gus had plenty of cash that he wouldn't keep in no bank. I watched him ride into town that night. I never figured he'd come back and catch me while I was robbing him."

"Then what?"

"He caught me in the parlor and tore into me like a raging bull. I tried to hold him off with my gun, but he just kept coming. I had to fire. Even then he kept coming.... There, I said it...Are you satisfied now?"

"No, you need to tell all this to Miss Ekberg."

"You can tell her."

"I'm afraid that wouldn't do much good."

"She's pretty as an angel, ain't she? I never figured on Ingrid being so god awful pretty."

"Don't pin this on her."

"I didn't say that, it's just"

"Yeah?"

"I've been writing her for the last two years. It was my pa's idea. He knew her kin back in Sweden. Wasn't any girl around here that...At least not that I was interested in."

"Well, Rod...So long."

"Wait, wait...I'll tell her everything...But it wasn't cold blooded, like you said, Wade. Would you tell my pa that for me?"

"Yes."

"You mean it?"

"You have my word."

ᴜᴜᴜᴜᴜᴜᴜ

I didn't stay through the hanging.

I learned Rod, as promised, had finally explained things to Miss Ekberg, and I reckon she finally saw what had happened in kind of a different light. Anyway, I heard she stayed on in Houston working at Christie's Café until she earned enough money to take the train back to her sister's in Wisconsin.

Texas ain't for everyone.

Who could blame her?

She was a good, brave girl. The kind of loving and loyal girl that a settling-down type of man could build a life with.

I'd like to think things worked out for her.

PERDITION
BIG SPRING TALE

"A closed mouth gathers no boots."
– Texas Proverb

IT WAS A LONG night under a thin blanket beneath a frosty moon. The dream was inevitable, I suppose. The day's events were still too fresh in my mind. The open range has thousands of tales to tell, and most fade into obscurity like raindrops in oceans of time.

Right before dusk I'd come across the grave of a cowboy killed by horse rustlers back in the day. This wasn't so unusual. The Texas plains were a source of clear and present danger.

The thing that made this poor soul's final resting place striking was it kindled an old tune in my mind's eye.

"Bury Me Not on the Lonely Prairie."

His fate was definitely lonely to me. It had snowed again that night, sticky wet snow that pine trees bent under. The slate-gray boulders were blanketed white.

I woke up lying under a frosty layer of snow. Early morning shivering is the worst kind. Badger was standing next to the smokey remains of the campfire. He was kind of shaking his way dry like a white-whiskered moose.

"Easy boy, I'll get us a fire going."

I'd gathered wood up last night, but it was just too wet. So, I snatched a small axe out of

a pack and headed over toward a little hill about forty yards away. I figured there was brush shielded from the northern winds on the far side of some boulders. It was dry enough to burn but there wasn't near enough of it.

The sun hadn't splashed through the misty clouds yet, but the snow was already melting to mud. There were some dead pine saplings on the ground by another set of boulders. I figured they would fire up as well.

Badger snorted up a racket and my back was to him.

Probably a squirrel and I hoped not a skunk.

It was a heap worse than that.

I dropped the axe and drew my Colt as I began sprinting back. The sun was peeking over the horizon, reflecting off the snow which glared into my eyes.

When I got my eyes focused I saw a fellow standing beside Badger, trying to cinch the saddle onto his back.

"Hey, hey you! Let that horse alone!"

He looked up and for a minute froze like he was unsure what to do. Then he put his foot in the stirrup. Badger was rearing but he didn't buck to keep the fellow off.

I won't make it in time.

I hated to risk a shot with Badger moving the way he was, but a man wouldn't last two days out here without a horse or supplies.

My first shot was high. This doesn't mean much—it's when bullets are bouncing at your feet they got your range. Badger was taking the spurs and sort of starting to move despite himself.

Another minute or so and they'd be out of pistol range.

I took a knee, held the Colt with both hands, and squeezed off a round slow and smooth while holding my breath.

It caught the fellow high on the leg.

He twisted around and tried to get a firm grip when Badger decided enough was enough and bucked him off into the snow. I couldn't tell if he had a gun but figured he must.

I dove behind a clump of bushes. There was a clearing between us and he was using a boulder for cover.

I fired again.

A small spray of snow told me I'd hit the boulder he was using for cover.

He's not shooting back.

Could be a trick.

If he was waiting for me to get anxious and slip up, that wasn't happening. I reloaded my Colt and looked to the right.. There was a way to circle without being seen and I'd surprise him from behind.

It took twice as long as it should have, but I ended up in frosted bushes behind him. He was laying sprawled out face-down in bloodstained snow.

I charged over to finish it.

There was a pistol lying beside him within easy reach.

I kicked it away and saw why he hadn't used it.

Most of the bleeding was coming from a gunshot wound in his lower back. He'd tried to bandage it with some cloth but it didn't matter. I picked up his pistol and saw it still had two rounds. I emptied them and threw his gun as far away as I could..

I had him covered and eased him over with my boot. He moaned and his eyes slid half open.

He shrugged then started shivering.

"I robbed a slew of banks but ain't never been a horse thief before."

"You best take it easy."

"Too late for that. Maybe it's better dying out here than hanging. I always said Dan Ketchum would never hang."

"Ketchum?"

"You heard of me, ain't you?"

"Yeah, I've heard of you."

"Everybody's heard of Dan Ketchum. Too bad, your shot ain't killing me. There's a thousand-dollar reward on me ever since I shot that U.S. Marshal in Tucson."

He coughed up some blood.

"Relax."

"That reward's fancier after the stage depot I hit yesterday. That fellow inside died hard. He could have just given me the money...But shot me in the back."

"Yeah."

"But I got him too. I turned and got him straight through the heart."

"You killed Larry Fisher?"

"I don't know his name, or the names of most men I've killed."

"How'd you get thirty miles from Big Spring without a horse?"

"My palomino tipped with all that snow coming down a few houses back."

"Yeah."

"I hated putting him down...He was a fine horse."

"Yeah."

"That's why I needed yours."

"I reckon there's a posse after you?"

"I ain't never stole no horse before, mister."

"Do you reckon you can hang on if I hoist you onto the saddle?"

"What for?"

"You need a doctor and Badger can carry us both."

"Closest doc is Big Spring."

"That's right."

"I'd never make it that far."

"You can try."

"No, if we run into that posse they'd string me up. I won't be hung."

'Well, I...."

"Mister, I ain't got but a few hours. I'm dead anyway. Let's stay here then you can collect that nice reward afterwards. I can't be lynched."

"Nobody's gonna lynch you, Ketchum."

"Give me your word."

"Yeah."

He was just hanging by a thread, but we had to try. The leg wasn't so bad but that bullet in his back was serious.

He passed out again.

I picked him up, laid him across Badger's back. Then I looped a rope around his body and tried to fix it so that he wouldn't slide so much. It wasn't going to be comfortable, but he wasn't feeling anything while unconscious.

"All right Badger, let's go."

Badger worked hard carrying both of us through all that slush. We were slow but steady.

It was almost three hours later before we came to the main Big Spring trail.

I spotted the posse just as we turned onto it.

There were five men loping along toward us with guns ready.

Doc Akers headed the procession, and he was the local dentist. And I recognized Terry Burrow and Fred Ellis right behind them. The pair of boys bringing up the rear didn't look familiar.

"Well, howdy, Wade."

"Hello, Doc."

"Well, boys, what'd I tell you? I said it was Wade Maverick."

"I'm pleased to meet you, Mr. Maverick, I'm Kyle Smith and this here's Larry Brown."

"Nice to meet you boys. Call me Wade."

Doc smirked. "Yes, sir, the minute you come into sight. I said, there's the Red Gun. It appears you're carrying quite a load, Wade."

"Yeah."

"What happened?"

"It's Dan Ketchum."

"Ketchum? No, he's supposed to be in Arizona."

"It's him."

"Let's see here," Doc said while checking a wanted leaflet. "Well, that is Ketchum! If that don't take their cake, this neighborhood's getting to be right outlaw unfriendly!"

"Is that so?'

"Well, maybe they'll change their tune about these parts after they find out what happened today…"

"Yeah?"

"Yeah, we set a county record with your help here, of course."

"Boys, you didn't need my help with Ketchum."

"What do you mean there, Wade? We didn't have the faintest notion Ketchum was anywhere near here."

"You didn't?"

"No, we were already on our way back to town."

'Wait, you mean you weren't looking for Ketchum?"

"Of course not."

"I thought you were a posse?"

"We are a posse. But we were hunting Tom Gwinup."

"Gwinup?"

Doc answered, "Yeah, you remember him, don't you? Gwinup robbed Harry Goldberg's general store, a couple of years back. He near killed old man Goldberg."

"Yeah, I uh…remember."

"Well, sir, he broke out of jail a week ago in Odessa, and what do you think he did? Gwinup headed straight for Big Spring, and he tried to pull another robbery."

"I see."

"Yeah, but this time he killed Larry Fisher while he was at it."

"Now, now, just wait a minute here, boys. You're telling me you're all after Tom Gwinup, and that you think he's responsible for the robbery at the stage depot last night?"

"Think? We know it, Wade. But there ain't no need to look for him anymore."

"What?'

Terry smiled. "We found him!"

"You did?"

"Yeah, just a couple of hours ago, hiding in a cabin over by Comanche Creek. We saw to it he won't be pulling no more holdups, neither. It isn't as if we didn't give Gwinup a trial."

"A trial?"

Doc said, "Well, there was no doubt about his being guilty, Wade. Seeing as there's no judge in Big Spring, we'd have to wait till next spring for a formal hanging. So, we sort of speeded things up a mite."

"You... you didn't string him up yourself."

Fred nodded. "We sure did. Yes sir! Justice for poor old Larry!"

"Now, boys, just hold your horses."

Doc gave me the side-eye. "Wade, what's that look for? What's done is done."

"Well, that's true enough, Doc."

Doc said, "What's the matter, Wade? Why you're as touchy as a sore-footed badger."

"Well, I don't know what to say."

Dan Ketchum hadn't been lying when he told me about robbing the depot and shooting Larry Fisher. You know, a man doesn't admit to something like that with one foot in the grave, unless it's the truth. As for Tom Gwinup, he'd always been rotten to the core. He'd gunned men down and beat on women.

But he hadn't killed Larry Fisher.

That's the one thing he didn't do.

Ketchum coughed faintly.

Doc observed, "Well, it seems Ketchum's still with us."

"Yeah. Well, I'd better get moving."

Fred asked, "Well, you want us to take him into town for you, Wade?"

"No, no, thanks. You see, I gave him my word to get him to a medical doctor."

"Why?"

"Well, he was afraid he might be lynched."

Doc shook his head. "We ain't got no grudge against Ketchum, Wade. Oh, he's a bad one all right, but he ain't never bothered us in Big Spring."

"Is that so?"

"Yes, like I said, we didn't even know he was in these parts."

"The problem, Doc, is Ketchum's the man who shot Larry Fisher."

"What's that? C'mon now, Wade. You're pulling my leg. You're trying to make us feel like we're just vigilantes for sorting out Tom Gwinup."

"All I'm saying is that Ketchum told me he held up the Big Spring stage depot last night and he killed the fellow in charge."

"You ain't serious?"

"I'm dead serious."

Terry said, "Wade, that don't make no sense. Why, it had to be Gwinup."

"What makes you so sure?"

Doc replied, "Well, we knew he broke jail and somebody said they thought they'd seen him in town yesterday. Now, let me see who.... Oh, it was Greg Spradling, I think...Yeah, yeah. We picked up his trail not far from the depot. It led right to that cabin on Comanche Creek where we found him."

"Did he confess to the robbery or the shooting?"

Doc proclaimed, "Why, you can't expect a man to admit that sort of thing when facing a hanging rope."

"Yeah, well, I'll see you."

"No, wait. Now, hold on now, Wade."

"What for?"

"Why, you just got to be wrong."

"You think I'm lying, Doc?"

"No, no, of course not, Wade. But everything pointed to Gwinup. Maybe Ketchum was just making that up, what he told you?"

"Well, how did he find out about the robbery then? He also told me he shot Larry right through the heart. Is that true?"

They shared nervous glances in response.

"So, how else would Ketchum know this?"

Doc answered, "Well, I... Now, Wade, you know we wouldn't have done anything if we weren't certain in our own minds that we were right."

"Yeah."

"Why, you know that...There's a slight chance we made a mistake. Well, I'm not saying so, but maybe...No. Well, even if we did, Gwinup deserved hanging. He deserved it for a long time."

"Yeah."

"Yes, that's what I'm getting at. We didn't do any harm, Wade, not really."

"You didn't do any harm, Doc?"

"Oh, of course not. But if you were to tell folks about Ketchum, well, they might not see it our way. Folks might reckon that we took the law into our own hands."

"So long, I'm taking Ketchum into town."

"So you won't say anything, will you?"

"Whatever he says after he gets there, that's up to him."

"Well, I know, Wade...But I mean..."

Then, a man's faint death rattle sounded from Badger's back.

I sighed, "You don't need to worry about Ketchum. He ain't gonna say nothing."

"Why?"

"Just take a look."

He was dying. I cut the rope that was holding him on Badger's back and carried him over to a dry space just off to the side of the trail. His body spasmed, and I felt the life ease out of his body just as I placed him on the ground.

Ketchum was right about one thing. Nobody would hang him.

Fred said, "I guess this saves your trip into Big Spring, Wade?"

"I was heading into town anyway, Fred."

"Oh?"

"I've come this far, I'll go the rest of the way."

Kyle spoke up for the first time "Well, I don't...Now, look here, Wade. Ketchum is dead."

"Yeah?"

"Well, then don't you see, there's nobody to say whether he was the one who killed Larry Fisher or not?"

"Nobody but Wade," Larry observed.

"That's right."

Doc spoke up. "Now, now, suppose we did go off half-cocked. Suppose we were kind of hasty with Gwinup. Well, we're sorry about it, but there's nothing we can do for him now."

"It seems you told me that before."

"Well, it's the truth, ain't it?"

"Sure."

Larry pleaded. "Well, then why get us into hot water? What's the point in telling folks that we kind of overstepped the mark?"

"Is that what you call kind of overstepping the mark?"

Doc added, "Well, it'd be different if Gwinup was innocent."

"Somehow I got the notion that he was."

"Oh, yes, of this robbery, maybe, but, well, he is…"

Kyle grunted, "I had a brother, Maverick…. He'd be alive today if it wasn't for Tom Gwinup."

"Is that why you strung him up, to avenge your brother?"

"No, no, of course not. We were just doing our duty as citizens. We thought he shot Larry Fisher."

"Well, I'll see you, boys."

There was a hard edge to Kyle's voice. "If Wade wants to try and make trouble, well, he ain't got no proof…It's his word against ours."

Larry added, "That's right. Kyle's right. We can even say that Gwinup confessed. Why, everybody in Big Spring will believe us."

"Well then, I reckon you boys got nothing to worry about."

Doc stammered, "Why, we ain't worried, Wade. Not really, of course we're not…I know you pretty well…We've been friends a long time. Why, you're not going to go out of your way to stir up a hornet's nest? I'm sure of that."

Kyle interrupted. "Well, I ain't so sure. Just a minute, Wade. You're not leaving here yet."

"I'm not, Kyle?"

"No, you're not. And boys, it's about time we start using our heads. If he goes into town and spreads this story around, they'll all believe it. Whatever Wade Maverick says, that's gospel…But he ain't going to say anything…That's right, he ain't…Because he ain't riding into Big Spring. He's turning around heading west."

"Is that so, Kyle?"

"I know you're quick on the draw, but there's five of us. No one's that fast."

"No, I reckon I'm not."

Larry said, "Now Kyle, nobody wants to get into a mix-up with Wade."

"What do you want? People to start saying we murdered Tom Gwinup. Murdered? Well, that ain't what we done at all."

I answered, "His family might disagree with you, Kyle, if they found out the truth about that holdup last night. And he's got a brother, too."

Larry said, "Well, maybe there is something in what Kyle says. But we can't stop Wade...Now, if he takes it upon himself..."

"We stopped Gwinup, didn't we?"

Kyle drew his pistol.

"But, Kyle..." Larry protested.

Doc ordered, "Put that gun away, Kyle."

"Sure, I'll put it away. After I'm sure that Maverick's riding east. And I'm warning you, Wade, don't you ever breathe about what Ketchum told you..."

"I don't care to be ordered around, Kyle."

"Then just keep away from Big Spring...Now move...I said..."

I held my ground.

I didn't know Kyle. This business with Gwinup had pushed him into deep water. I watched his jaw muscles tighten up and I saw a little bead of sweat form between his eyes, and for a minute nobody said anything.

But I knew Doc, Terry and Fred.

And then Doc Akers shoved forward.

"I told you to put it away, Kyle. Wasn't what we already done today bad enough? You want to kill somebody else?"

"We done nothing wrong! Get that through your skull, Doc. Gwinup deserved to hang and we hung him."

"What about Wade?"

"Suppose he deserves being shot?"

Doc roared, "That's horse crap and you know it! That gun you're holding just proves how wrong we were this morning. If we'd been right, you wouldn't need it."

"Shut up!"

Doc went on, "If we'd been right, we wouldn't be standing here feeling ashamed. Even you feel ashamed. That's why you don't want nobody to hear about it, Kyle. That's why you're threatening Wade here."

"And I'll make good on that threat too!"

Doc shook his head. "No you won't. Because we're going into Big Spring and telling them what happened. We're going to take our medicine."

"You've all gone loco!"

Doc replied, "And it ain't just because Gwinup didn't kill Larry Fisher, even if he had. Well, it still wouldn't have been right. I reckon we wouldn't have found out so quick, but we'd have found out sooner or later."

Kyle's face went red. "You know what's the matter, you've all got a yellow streak a yard wide down your back. You were all just as giddy to string up Gwinup."

Doc sighed. "Kyle, do you know what magnanimous means?"

"Why does that matter?"

"You should read up on it, because if Wade here wasn't magnanimous, he could have killed you three times before you could blink. There's a reason they call him the Red Gun."

Terry and Fred had had enough. They nodded to me in apology and turned for town. Larry lingered and glanced at Kyle then rode off as well.

Larry yelled back, "Doc, you coming along?"

"Yeah, just a sec. Kyle, this ain't you, c'mon let's go home."

Kyle sighed and holstered his pistol.

The pair of them rode off for Big Spring.

Kyle kept yelling at them until they were out of sight

"You're all crazy fools, we didn't do a bad thing. What's the matter with ending a killer like Gwinup? Hey, why can't you all see we did Texas a favor?"

I picked up Ketchum's body and laid it across Badger's back.

We rode for Big Spring.

There had been more than enough killing of late.

WHITE OWL
ADOBE WALLS TALE

"An ignorant fella is hell-bent on proving his limitations."
– Montana Proverb

DAWN'S FIRST COLORS FLOWED through a twisted live oak grove east of Adobe Walls.

There are some things you can't unsee.

It was an Indian.

I couldn't tell if he was dead or not.

The bloody trail he'd left behind and the way he was sprawled out motionless among the swirling leaves was bad, real bad.

He was dead all right and it was an ugly death. Someone had killed him slow, cold and cruel. He'd been shot through both knees to start. He was trying to crawl away when he got finished off...

I was just about to dismount.

I felt I was being watched.

I pulled the saddle gun out of its scabbard and noted Badger's ears and head. Whoever it was, they were in a thick grove of trees to the south.

I wheeled Badger to face them.

A squaw stepped out of the trees. Her eyes swept back and forth between the body and me.

They are both Comanche.

I lowered the carbine.

She had her hand on a sheathed knife and walked slowly toward me. Her eyes were dark, moist and determined. She halted ten yards away.

Brave woman.

I pointed to myself and then the body and shook my head. "I didn't do this. Do you understand, I didn't kill him."

She looked me straight in the eyes. "I understand white man talk."

"Uh, yeah, is this your husband?"

"Yes."

"What was his name?"

"Standing Bear."

"Standing Bear," I repeated softly.

She took her hand off her knife handle.

"I'm Wade Maverick. I'm just riding through, not law or a soldier."

"Law much strong for whites."

"You know who killed your husband?"

"No."

"You know why your husband was killed?"

"No. Standing Bear good husband, much heart, big, strong."

I began to dismount. "I will help you bury him."

"No!" she said sharply.

"All right." I pulled back up in the saddle.

"Indian bury husband," she said in a softer tone.

"Well, I'll go."

It didn't seem right leaving her there by herself, but that's what she wants.

ՍՍՍՍՍՍՍՍ

At dusk, a thin curl of smoke drifted out of the stone chimney of the Three Falls Saloon.

It was one of them beautiful red, purple, and orange Texan sunsets.

Stinnett hadn't changed a lick.

"Well, hello there Wade, it's good to see you"

"Good to see you, Matt."

"You know, I'd reckoned maybe you'd wandered off the edge of the Earth and fell to your doom."

"Town looks good. Even though it's unclear you know the earth is round."

He laughed. "Same old ramshackle rookeries, no real buildings yet. So far though, the Comanches are calm and the creek don't rise."

"What creek?"

"Fair point, that!"

We shook.

Matt Stevenson owned the only saloon in town. He'd been a cowpuncher and we'd been on more than one roundup together. Then a bad fall from a wild stallion cracked his back.

"How was the trip?"

"Long and dry."

"You're back for branding season out to the Yancy Ranch?"

"That I am."

"That kicks off in a day or so?"

"Yeah."

"Beer?"

"No, give me a bottle of Irish and leave the bottle please."

"Jameson's? All right…. You…Uh, you good Wade?"

"Yeah, I need a drink, some enchiladas and a bath."

"No offense, Wade, but I ain't ever seen you drink much whiskey, and never more than one."

"I'll tell you what's the trouble, Matt. Disgust for my fellow man."

"Hell, I'll drink to that."

"But I reckon I'll get over it."

"What happened?"

"It was on the way in today, I found a dead Indian. His squaw came along about the same time. It was rough to watch, that's all."

"Men die like flies in these parts, and their womenfolk grieve.... There must be more to this, Wade...We've both seen the elephant, and heard the owl."

"Yeah."

"I don't have to tell you what Comanches are capable of on a raid."

"Well it was just like that. He was killed a piece at a time. Somebody had shot out both knees so he'd crawl. Then he was gutshot to suffer, and in the end scalped alive."

Matt shrugged. "The Comanche would also have cut his pecker off and left it in his mouth."

"I know that, Matt. Like I said, my disgust is for all of us...It wasn't until they'd had their fun that they finished him off.... His squaw saw what had happened to him, so anyway..."

A man raised his voice at the bar. "Everyone hush. I'm listening to a funny story!" Then he focused intently back on me.

Who is this fool?

I was hot, "Is it my funny story you're listening to?"

"Yeah, that's right. Do you object?"

"You have some special interest in Indians?"

"I do at that. It's a good story. Go on, how does it end?"

"It hasn't ended yet."

"I could end it better for you.... If it was me out there, that squaw would have met the same fate as her buck!"

"Is that's so?"

"Yeah, I hate Indians. I kill them. That's mighty near all I got on my mind. I enjoy killing them. I hate Indian lovers, too...I'm Art Rutzen, what's your name, mister?"

Matt cut in. "Hobble your lip, Rutzen. We heard enough."

"It's a free country. A man can't say his piece?"

Matt answered, "Yes, you can, but I run the only saloon in Hutchinson County and I'm also free to cut you off. I'm also trying to save your life."

Rutzen cackled. "Aren't you in the wrong line of work to push teetotaling?"

Matt shrugged. "No, keep this up and I imagine you die of lead poisoning. Then I'd have to drag your body out of my place."

"Are you threating me barkeep?"

"Actually no, Rutzen, I'm letting you know this fellow here you're jawing at is Wade Maverick, and he's in one bear of a mood."

Rutzen eyed me again. "You're the Red Gun?"

I didn't reply.

He hesitated and swallowed then the fire was back in his eyes. "That still don't give you a right to tell me who I can hate."

"No. That's your business. Just don't bore me with it."

"Well, I'm gonna go on killing Indians, Mr. Maverick. I've been it doing for seventeen years."

"That's a long time, Mr. Rutzen."

His eyes flared again, possessed with hate. "It seems like no more than yesterday over by Adobe Walls. I come back from hunting one time. My wagon was burnt. They'd taken turns with my pretty wife and her back was stuck full of arrows. They bashed my infant daughter's head on a tree. My baby son was carried off.... They was Comanches.... So Mr. Maverick, go ahead and gun me down, Mr. Red Gun. It don't change a thing...This is between me and the Comanches. I'm gonna kill them till the day I die!"

I sighed, "There's been enough bloodshed around here, Rutzen."

"You've had enough, Rutzen," Matt said.

"My money's no good here?"

"I ain't saying you can't drink, just no more here tonight."

Rutzen cackled. "I don't know what's worse—being killed or cut off from whiskey."

He staggered out the door.

∪∪∪∪∪∪∪∪

Dawn's light flickered off the brass mantle of my bed. Matt Stevenson was kind enough to let me bunk out in a spare room upstairs. The smell of fresh coffee boiling wafted upstairs.

He was polishing down the counter of his bar with a pencil behind his ear when I made it downstairs.

"Morning, Matt."

"Good morning."

"Well you must have been good and saddle sore there, compadre."

"Yeah."

"I never knew you to let sunrise catch you snoring?"

"It don't happen often. I reckon it was that fancy bed."

"Yeah."

"What's that look for?"

"Well...I just never figured to see you all settled down with a pencil behind your ear."

"Everyone's got to settle down someday, Wade."

"I suppose."

"Wade, haven't you once found anywhere you wanted to stay?"

"At first, just about every place seems solid. Then in a bit I get to ponderin' there might be somethin' better down the road."

"But it's never there, is it?"

"It's always good, anywhere for a little while."

"Yeah, there are times I envy your freedom."

"So far so good."

"There has to have been a lady or two that tempted an old bachelor to see the error of his ways?"

"Yeah, long story."

"I'm all ears."

"Hmm, you ever been up to Colorado?"

"Was there a girl in Colorado?"

"It's gorgeous country. Snowcapped mountains, evergreen valleys, and deep blue lakes."

"Yes, and...?"

"The thing is maybe I'm one pickle short of a barrel, but I still prefer good old West Texas."

"Why? It's nothing but drought, red dust, wind and endless sky?"

"Not to me. There's a sense of freedom to the open range I never found in crowds or towns anywhere. I don't answer to clocks and life is timeless—it's like the stars at night, crisp and bright. It's little things like reading by a campfire as coyotes wail at the moon, the distant call of a calf for its mother, or the smell of greasewood after a thunderous downpour."

"Heck, I remember them prairies days. The frontier is fading fast."

"That it is."

"What if you found a gal who had the same wanderlust?"

"That is one heck of a question."

"They are out there, you know. Gals like that."

"Possibly."

"Coffee?"

"Please."

He reached back and poured scalding black liquid into a tin cup. "There's likely a morning biscuit or two left and some blackstrap molasses."

I was still scraping the last bit of a biscuit into the molasses when there was a knock on the door. It was a lanky, freckle-faced, towheaded button. His young face was flush with excitement.

"Mr. Stevenson! Mr. Stevenson?"

Matt answered, "Morning, Bobby, what can I do for you?"

"I was stocking the shelves at the store when I saw her out the window! She's still there!"

"Relax, son. Who is she?"

"A squaw! A real-life Comanche squaw, and she speaks English some!"

"You're saying there's Comanche in town?"

"No, sir. She's standing there waiting just outside of town."

I asked, "How do you know she speaks English?"

"She was yelling out asking for a Mr. Maverick."

"She was?"

"Yes, I swear it. Pa sent me over to warn folks in case there's trouble."

"Just her?" Matt asked.

"Yes. Is it a raid?"

I shook my head, "There hasn't been a raid in quite a spell, and Comanches on a raid don't stop to announce themselves. I'll go talk to her."

Matt said, "I'll come with since she likely ain't alone."

"I can sort it out, Matt."

"No, Comanches is serious. I'm coming with. I can't bust broncos no more, but I can still ride and shoot."

ᴜᴜᴜᴜᴜᴜᴜ

She was waiting patiently, with her hand on her knife sheath again, just outside of town. We didn't see any other Indians around.

"Brave woman to come to town alone," I observed.

Matt replied, "Yeah, but half the Comanche Nation could be hid out in those ridges west of town."

He checked the action on his lever gun.

I added, "I reckon she must have had some pretty good reason to come all this way."

"Yeah."

"Well, she's moving out into the clearing."

"I don't like this," Matt said.

"You want to wait here?"

"I didn't say that, Wade."

"Look, keep me covered with the Winchester, I'll go talk to her."

I made the sign for peace and she nodded.

"Maverick," she said.

"Yes, you came alone from Adobe Walls?"

"We talk."

"How did you know I was here in Stinnett?"

She smiled. "We know all in our lands."

"Well, we meet again. I don't even know your name?"

She smirked. "My name no important."

"My friend says that there must be more Indians with you?."

Yes, back there." She pointed to the ridge. "White Owl is brother. He no make talk. He wait."

"All right."

"Just the two of you?"

"No other. Most my people go new home, Oklahoma."

"All right."

She pointed to town. "White man who kill Standing Bear is here."

"How do you know this?"

"After husband dead, White Owl track white man to here."

"I see."

"In my village man who kills other Indian we kill to punish. Is same with whites?"

"Yes, mostly."

"Why are you asking for me?"

"Maverick see Standing Bear killed bad."

"Yes."

"You find, you make prisoner, you kill him."

"It's not that simple, who is this white man?"

"He wear black hat. He ride black horse."

"That could be many men. Did you or the brother see the killing?"

"No."

"Our rules are we must be sure to punish. Understand?"

"If no sure, you no kill this white man?"

"That's right."

"White Owl track. No other tracks from where Standing Bear killed."

"Then you give us white man, we kill."

"No, we can't do that."

"This much bad! My people much angry."

"I'm sorry."

"White man big enemy! We no make peace. We wait, we kill."

She turned and walked off into the prairie with her head held high.

I walked back and filled Matt in.

He asked, "Do you reckon they will see this through?"

"Yeah, she meant it."

"Rutzen has a black hat and horse."

"I figured."

"What do we do?"

"I don't know. We can't prove it unless he confesses. I'd want revenge too if it were my kin."

"The law ain't going to try no white man for killing an Indian, especially a Comanche, with no witnesses. Heck, Rutzen could claim he was attacked first."

"Yeah.'

"There's too many guns in town for them to risk a raid."

"Probably. I reckon maybe we send for some cavalry and have them escort him out."

"I don't like this fellow bringing this Injun trouble to Stinnett."

"Rutzen might be innocent."

"You believe that, Wade?"

"No."

'Well, he keeps a room by the livery stable. Let's tell him the score."

∪∪∪∪∪∪∪∪

Rutzen was still feeling the effects from last night's whiskey back in his room.

"Rutzen, we need talk to you."

"Come on in."

Matt said, "There are some Indians just outside of town."

"Why does everyone in these parts seem so mighty fond of Indians?"

"I'm fond of keeping Stinnett from burning in a blood raid, Rutzen."

I said, "These Comanche claim a man recently killed one of them over to Adobe Walls."

"So what?"

"Was it you that killed that Comanche?"

"I killed plenty of Indians the last seventeen years."

I asked, "Did you kill that one yesterday?"

"What if I did?"

"We'd inform the county marshal."

He snorted. "Even if it was me, no marshal would try a white man for killing a Comanche. Hell, you might as well arrest someone for stepping on a worm."

Matt said, "The law is not your problem, Rutzen."

"Other than you cutting me off from whiskey, I ain't got no problems."

"The Comanche think a man fitting your description did this, they want blood, and one of them can identify you."

"That ain't proof."

"They've tracked you here, don't care about proof, and are waiting for you."

"What's that?"

Matt said, "That's right. So you stay in this town. You set one foot outside of Stinnett and those Comanche will kill you good and slow."

"Why are you helping me?"

Matt snapped, "We aren't. I think you murdered that Comanche. We want you out of town. We'll send for soldiers to escort you out. It's the only way."

"Don't be sure of that, boys. Don't be so sure of that."

◡◡◡◡◡◡◡◡

The next few days passed in peace. They held a town meeting and implemented a curfew. The men of Stinnett were armed at all times and we posted a lookout in the church steeple. The women and children were instructed not to stray far from town.

There was an almost palpable tension to the air.

Rutzen, for all his bile and bravado, seemed to sober up. I can't blame him. If you've ever fought the Comanche, they are as deadly as can be. I've never seen better horsemen. They don't even need saddles and stirrups. They can make a horse do just about anything using only their knees and feet. It's hard to believe some of the bloodthirsty tales from both sides back in the day. I reckon a lot of them are true. Either way, only a fool would want a Comanche blood debt hanging over his head.

Then, things happened fast.

It was about three o'clock in the afternoon and time for me to head off to the ranch for the start of branding season. Matt had sent for the cavalry and we figured maybe there was a chance Stinnett could be free of Rutzen without bloodshed.

Once more, little Bobby Turner broke the news. He'd come sprinting over, red-faced, huffing and puffing from his father's general store.

"Mr. Stevenson! Mr. Stevenson, my pa told me to tell you Mr. Rutzen just left town!"

Matt shook his head. "That fool should know better."

I said, "We best fetch him back."

"Why? Let them end it."

"Matt, this could still go bad. Let's get Rutzen back here before there's more blood that triggers a raid."

∪∪∪∪∪∪∪∪

We mounted up quick and went after him. Matt ordered the town to shelter up and be ready for anything.

We were about two miles west of town when Matt said, "I reckon them wooded hills up ahead would be a fine spot to set up an ambush."

"I don't know, if it were Apaches I'd agree. Comanches like open range horseback fights."

"Yeah, wait a minute. Did you just see that rider by that gap in them salt cedars to the south?"

"Yes, but Rutzen's likely headed back north or east, I would."

"It's that squaw, Wade!"

She saw us and rode back into the trees.

"Come on!"

We galloped in pursuit.

This made no sense but we had to try.

Comanche women are also excellent riders and Indian ponies can usually run circles around our horses.

Even Badger.

We somehow eventually caught her. Actually we didn't. She just eventually stopped, turned and faced us with a grim smile.

"You kill me now, Maverick? I sing my death song and glad see my husband in spirit lands."

"No, why did you run?"

She smiled. "So you follow. Now White Owl kill bad white man."

So there was just the two of them...

She'd decoyed us perfectly.

As if on cue, rifle shots and pistol blasts came from the wooded hills to the northwest.

Matt said, "I reckon that's Rutzen and that Comanche stalking each other in them hills."

"Yeah."

She was positively beaming now. "White Owl get revenge, you will see."

We left her there and rode hard for those hills.

We still had to try...

ՍՍՍՍՍՍՍՍ

"Rutzen! Rutzen!"

He was lying on his back, shot through the chest, in a dark pool of blood.

There were thick thorn thickets around him and wooded boulders further uphill.

His voice was fading. "Here.... I.... I'm here."

We dismounted and tried to help him pass easy.

"Just relax, if you can."

"I gots me another Comanche, but he got me too..."

"Where is he, Rutzen?"

"There.... Right.... Over in them boulders by that big oak."

Matt stayed with Rutzen while I stalked over for White Owl.

He'd been shot right through the head.

White Owl was young. Not much more than a boy.

His skin is white.

I heard a horse approaching.

It was the squaw.

Her eyes were moist looking down on White Owl.

I said, "White Owl wasn't your real brother."

"No, my real brother killed by bluecoats as a baby."

"Yeah."

"Chief give mother white baby. Call him little White Owl.
He grow to be powerful warrior. He good brother.

"White man die?"

"He will very soon."

"I go now, Maverick."

She rode off into the sunset.

∪∪∪∪∪∪∪∪

Matt was calling for me as I walked back to them.

"Wade? Wade, you good?"

Rutzen wheezed. "I killed him, right?"

"Yeah, Rutzen."

"Good!"

"He was still a boy, just about eighteen or so."

Rutzen coughed his last breath. "That's just about right. By now my own son would have been just about eighteen."

The light went out of Rutzen's eyes and Matt closed them. Then he paused to look at the blood on his hands from Rutzen's face.

I was so sick to my stomach I retched all over.

"Wade, what is it? We both seen much worse than this."

"Maybe, maybe not, Matt."

"How's that, now?"

"White Owl was the spitting image of Art Rutzen."

"What?"

"Yeah."

"Wait, wait do you mean...?"

"Yes, I'm sure of it."

"Oh my god."

"Yeah."

"Well,...oh my...Well, I... I reckon it's best neither one knew."

"Yeah."

"All this bloody hate, Wade."

"Well, at least we can bury them together."

Quicksilver Butterfield Tale

"If you want to liven up the conversation, just say the right thing, the wrong way."
– **Utah Proverb**

THE BUTTERFIELD TRAIL LEADS over the crest of Guadalupe Mountains and then down the southern slope. The town was one of those rinky-dink places maps often miss. It was founded on fanciful prospects of easy money from nearby silver mining. The problem was no one had found silver here in ages, and the only easy money here was made by folks who sold pickaxes and mining pans for a pretty penny.

That's why you couldn't barely see Butterfield until you were already there, that and the clouds. There always seemed to be a mess of thick foggy marshmallow clouds along the side of

Butterfield, and by the time you got through them you likely already passed this little fly speck of a town.

Badger and I got in early one afternoon and I barely recognized the place. The outskirts hadn't changed in the decade since my last time through. Whitewashed loose timber frame houses with broken windows.

Front Street actually looked like a real town though. Butterfield might never be one of them truly important towns like Abilene, Chicago, Dodge City, or New York, but it was booming now. That's not to say it was anything particularly enduring. For example, when my pa was in short pants Cahawba was still the capital of Alabama. The locals decided it flooded far too much and left while taking the title of capital along.

That's one thing Butterfield had going for it. No chance of flood. Like most of West Texas, it was big blue sky, dusty winds and could go years without real rain.

Regardless, Meachum's Sundry store was open as was a new bank and they even had a post office. Why they also had two saloons, a slew of stores, and even two hotels now.

Is this place turning into a real town?

I saw what I came for. The sign on the old courthouse said Union Pacific Railroad Butterfield Office. There were boxes on the desk inside, but the room was empty.

"Ah, howdy, mister."

"Howdy."

"Mind handing me that box?"

"Sure."

"Yeah, thanks."

"Ah, you're cleaning out the office, huh?"

"That's right."

Well, I reckon there's plenty of vacancies in Butterfield, right?"

"Yeah, add one more to the list."

"Hold up, what, you're leaving town?"

"I wasted five weeks here, mister. Five weeks."

"I'm sorry."

"Butterfield doesn't deserve a railroad and they ain't getting one."

"Well, I was figuring on signing up with the railroad. I've laid track before and I thought, *Well, I heard the new line was coming through here.*"

"You heard wrong, mister."

"Yeah."

"Well, I'm sorry for your troubles, mister. There's plenty of other folks here who should be sorry. They gave me their word I'd have the right of way, free and clear."

He left me in the empty office and I stepped outside onto the boardwalk.

"Wade! Wade Maverick!"

"Huh?"

Over here in the barbershop! It's me, Doc Jenkins!"

"What? Oh! Oh, hello, Doc!"

"Come on in here!"

"Oh, well sure!"

"Doc, what in the thunder are you doing on a wheelchair?"

"I fell off my horse a few month back, I don't need it so much no more."

"Yup, we had to send for Doc Sullivan over to El Paso. He says I broke my leg. But, I

doubt that quack knows a broken leg from a bunion. If you ask me, he's keeping me off my feet, so's to steal all my patients."

"Oh, well, Doc, broken leg needs rest."

"Hey, sit down, Wade. Take a seat."

"Thanks. I was good and surprised to see the courthouse still open. I thought they'd moved the county seat over to El Paso."

"Yeah, those slithering politicians in El Paso bribed the legislature. They surely did. But we'll get the county seat back again, just you wait and see. Meantime, we're using the courthouse for a city hall. I'm the mayor now, Wade."

"Oh, congratulations."

"What about you? What brought you to Butterfield after all this time? I hope you ain't just wandering through."

"Well, Doc. I was aiming to sign up laying tracks for the railroad, but since they ain't coming this way..."

"Who gave you that notion?"

"Why, that fellow at the rail office..."

"Norris, Frank Norris? Don't pay no mind to him."

"Well, he does works for the railroad."

"Yes, but he ain't never wanted the line to go through Butterfield no how. I bet El Paso is paying him off."

"Really?"

"That's why he's been looking for an excuse to get out of our contract. He figures the Bonnie trouble gets him off the hook."

"Bonnie?"

"Silver Bonnie. You remember her, Wade, Bonnie Drexel."

"Oh, Bonnie Drexel. Of, course. I thought she'd moved away."

"No such luck."

"She's still squatting on the old Drexel silver mine like a hen guarding eggs. Lord knows there ain't no silver in that mine. There barely was in the first place."

"What's Bonnie got to do with the railroad?"

"Well, the railroad route's been surveyed to go through her property. Butterfield agreed to secure all the right-of-ways the railroad required. We're willing to pay her a good price."

"Bonnie want's more?"

"Worse. Old Bonnie refuses to sell at any price. She won't listen to anyone anymore and shoots off her shotgun if anyone comes on her land!"

I laughed. "No one's been hurt, right?"

"No, but Bonnie just sets there around the clock, right by the window, with her shotgun.

Anybody comes on her land, is trying to steal her mine, so she shoots. She's a plumb crazy old bird!"

"I don't know about that, Doc. Maybe Bonnie's livin' in the past some. She got quite a past too, if I recall right. I remember about her weddin' to Sam Drexel. He put down a street of silver dollars all around the church. You remember that?"

"Yes, well, that's long past...I sent for Clint Drexel."

"Clint Drexel?"

"Yeah, he's a relative of Sam's, a distant cousin or somethin' like that, but a relative. We done paid his fare all the way out from Chicago."

"Chicago? You don't say, has he seen Bonnie yet?"

"That's where he is right now. He's a fancified lawyer, and not the kind to put up with any malarkey!"

"I see."

We were interrupted by a pudgy duded-up middle-aged man with an indoor pallor. His fancy suit was caked in mud and he was pale, sweating and red in the face.

Doc called out, "Well, Mr. Drexel, back so soon? I didn't see you ride up."

"I didn't ride! I walked!"

But you...rode out not an hour...Don't tell me that horse of mine threw you, too. I..."

"The horse was fine. Where will I find Marshal Teague?"

"What?"

"I'm charging that old battleaxe with attempted murder!"

"Bonnie?"

"Yes, Bonnie! She ought to be locked up!"

Doc sighed. "She wouldn't sign over the right-of-way, huh? Not even for you, her own kin."

"I didn't get a chance to discuss it. She shot at me point-blank!"

Doc replied, "Well, I reckon she plumb didn't know who you were, Mr. Drexel."

"I told her who I was! Right after that, she ordered I grab earth and fired."

"Well, don't look like she hit you."

"It was a miracle she didn't."

I spoke up. "I doubt that it was attempted murder, sir."

"Who the hell are you?" Drexel roared.

"No offense."

He was still good and hot.

"Why should I give a hoot what you think?"

"I'm just saying, I've known Mrs. Drexel since the back during the Comanche raids. I've seen her shoot. If she wanted you dead, you'd already be six feet under."

"What's your name to preach to a lawyer what constitutes attempted murder?"

"My name is Maverick, Wade Maverick."

The man's face went stark white as his voice cracked. "The Red Gun?...Oh...I...I meant no offense, Mr. Maverick...It's just I never been shot at before."

I placated him with an open palm. "None taken, I don't care to be shot at neither."

Doc slammed his palm to his forehead. "Regardless, we gotta do somethin', and fast. If Butterfield don't have that right-of-way by tomorrow, Norris, the railroad man, will leave town without a signed contract. Then the railroad will just go through El Paso, which'll just about finish Butterfield now and for good."

He was so agitated he stood right up out of the wheelchair, walked over and kicked a pebble in the dusty street.

"Doc sit down, your leg?"

"It's near healed, but Butterfield won't recover if we don't get the railroad!"

I said, "Oh, c'mon now, there has to be some way of explainin' things to Bonnie, Doc."

"I could throw her in jail?"

"A little old lady?"

"Well, say, maybe there's another path."

"Right."

"Somebody she trusted, someone everyone respects with no axe to grind, maybe she'd listen to him."

I didn't care for the new gleam in his eyes.

"Now, wait a minute, Doc."

"Mr. Drexel, are those papers still ready to sign?"

"Yes."

"Then please give them to Wade."

"Now, this ain't my affair, Doc."

"Now, I know you, Wade. You wouldn't let us all down, not at a time like this. Go on, Mr. Drexel, give him the papers."

"Now, hold your horses."

"We'll never forget what you're doin', Wade. The whole town of Butterfield will be in your debt. Just get her to sign them—the places are marked with an X."

"Doc, but...I was just passing through for work...I can't..."

ᴗᴗᴗᴗᴗᴗᴗ

The next thing I knew, I was ridin' up to the Drexel mine. Bonnie's house was next to the main shaft, about two hundred yards off the old dusty road.

I slid down off Badger and tried the gate. The padlock was big enough to protect the Austin Mint.

Well, I simply had no choice but climb over the fence. Dusk was wrestling the sun down across the horizon.

I thought through my next step.

The front door was in plain view. Sneaking up on Mrs. Drexel could be fatal. So, I took cover behind a massive oak tree by the cabin door and called out.

A saddle gun fired into the air from the cabin.

"Get off my land or die, mister! Last warning!"

"It's me, Mrs. Drexel, Wade Maverick, please put that gun away...It's Wade!"

"Wade Maverick?"

"Yes, ma'am, it's me."

"Leave now, Wade. You were always a nice young fellow, I'd hate to shoot you."

"Mrs. Drexel, I'm an old friend coming over to catch up with you."

"All my friends is long buried. Everyone in Butterfield just wants my mine!"

Poor thing.

Old age ain't for the timid.

I sure hope I'm right.

"I am your friend, ma'am, and not from Butterfield. We survived the Comanche together and I was a button at your wedding. I'm coming to see you. Shoot if you must!"

"I guess there's no stopping you."

She opened the door.

"How are things, Mrs. Drexel?"

"Well, not so bad. If you close that door, I'll put some coffee to boil."

She placed the rifle back over the mantle.

"You called my bluff, Wade." She grinned. "As if I could ever shoot you."

"Coffee sounds bully."

"The fact of the matter is, Wade, I've been workin' the northern shaft lately. I found a vein that looks right promising. The Drexel Mine will soon be going full force again!"

"Do you truly believe that?"

"I do. Why shouldn't I? Sam and me took good money out of this earth. It's simply a matter of locating it."

She poured the scalding black coffee.

"Thank you."

"Haven't these hills been mined dry?"

"Drink your coffee, Wade."

"Thanks."

"There's nothing goes on in this town that I don't get wind of. I ain't lived here forty years for nothing."

"Well, Doc Jenkins maintains Butterfield needs the railroad, needs it to survive."

"Doc's a sly one, Wade. He pulls stunts like that wheelchair so folks underestimate the critter in his blood."

"Is that fair Ma'am? He's the mayor and maybe he wants the town to thrive?"

"Wade, do you mean to tell me in all your wanderings you never come across greedy politicians?"

"I didn't say that."

"I got no objection to a Butterfield railroad. I could use it myself to haul it all out when I strike a rich vein. But the line don't have to go through my property."

"In mountain country like this, railroads don't have much choice. Other routes would cost a whole lot more money than Union Pacific's willing to pay."

"Well, that ain't my problem. All I care about is the Drexel. And they not laying any tracks across it. Sam and I built this up from dirt. My children were born here. My Sam and some of them are buried on my lands."

"All right, Mrs. Drexel, I understand. Thanks for the coffee."

"It's good to see you, Wade."

"Oh, I reckon I ought to warn you. Your cousin's talking about putting you in jail."

"He ain't my real cousin. And as for locking me up, he'll have to find somebody to come out here and arrest me first."

The door kicked open.

Marshal Teague and Clint Drexel stormed in and grabbed the rifle from over the fireplace.

Bonnie cried, "What?"

I snapped, "What's going on here, Drexel?"

"This is a fair legal arrest. Thanks to you, Mr. Maverick, the marshal here was able to serve it."

Marshal Teague slapped handcuffs onto the table. "Right, Mr. Drexel."

She gave me a look of incredulous disbelief. "Wade, oh Wade, how could you say the things you said and do this? You knew my Sam and my boys."

"Mrs. Drexel, I...swear I didn't know they were doing this...I didn't know."

"Wade, of all the low-down...keeping me occupied so these varmints can slither in here."

"I didn't, it's not true!"

Fierce old Mrs. Bonnie Drexel was now sobbing like a lonely little old lady who had lived too long.

It broke my heart for my part in it.

Marshal Teague unshackled the cuffs.

Mrs. Drexel stood up straight. "I ain't one of them girls from China Lady Saloon. I'm Silver Bonnie Drexel! I was farming this soil, fighting the Comanche, and raising my boys when all of you was still nursing from your mama's! When I go to jail, I go under my own power."

ʊʊʊʊʊʊʊ

It was about eight o'clock when we got back to Butterfield. I stopped off at the Silverbug Hotel long enough to get me a room, then skipped supper as I headed over to Doc Jenkin's house.

He was sitting in the living room eating a box of hard candy when I got there. "Come on in, Wade. How'd you make out? Did she sign on the dotted line?"

"No."

He offered me a piece of candy.

I shook my head.

"Well, now don't feel too bad, Wade. I figured you wouldn't have much luck either. Mr. Drexel agreed and went ahead and got that warrant brought up."

"I know."

"Huh?"

"I was there when the marshal arrested her. She thinks I was in on it, with him and Drexel."

"That's a pity, but don't you worry. I'll see she finds out the truth."

"I should have just minded my own business from the beginning."

"You did the town a big favor. Butterfield's much obliged."

"Yeah."

"You know, hiring Clint Drexel was just about the slickest notion I ever pulled."

"Maybe so, but you haven't got the right-of-way yet."

"We'll get it, Wade."

"You didn't have to have to jail her. That attempted murder charge won't ever stick."

"He's not charging her with anything, Wade."

"What?"

"It's merely a question of whether she's still got her faculties. That's what the hearing will be about."

"You mean, he's claiming she's crazy?"

"No, you said yourself she was peculiar."

"I said she lived in the past, that's all. She's had a life worth remembering."

"Well, in her case, it's up to Judge Mathis to decide."

"Doesn't there need to be medical testimony and a sanity hearing?"

Doc Jenkins revealed a wolf-toothed smile. "Yep. Drexel subpoenaed me this evening."

This just isn't right.

They were railroading Mrs. Drexel the whole time...

And, I helped their scheme.

Doc exclaimed, "Drexel's her only relative. He looked up Texas state law. It says the nearest relative can demand a sanity hearing if there's sufficient cause."

"You take that mine away from her, she'll die of a broken heart."

"Now, Wade. You said yourself this wasn't none of your business."

I was tempted to break this old weasel's other leg.

I bit my tongue.

"Fair enough. Good night, Doc. I'll see you later."

ᘮᘮᘮᘮᘮᘮᘮ

Judge Mathis held the sanity hearing two days later.

"Now, Mrs. Drexel, for the record, you admit firing a shotgun at various persons who have approached your place of residence."

"I've shot at people trying to get into my Drexel silver mine, if that's what you mean. Maybe I put a good scare on them, but I was just aiming to scare and didn't hit a soul."

"Right. Now, how often has this occurred?"

"Whenever trespassers came for my silver. Is that crazy, judge?"

The courtroom burst out into laughter.

Judge Mathis slammed down his gavel. "Order, order in the court. This is a serious matter.... Now, well, surely you admit this behavior of yours isn't exactly normal."

"It's what I normally do."

"Order, come to, everyone!... What I mean is the average person doesn't use firearms on unarmed visitors."

"The average person don't own the largest silver mine in Texas. I do."

Folks were falling out of their chairs in hysterics laughing now.

"Uh, yeah."

Clint Drexel cut in, "If I may, Your Honor."

"Go ahead."

"This is sadly the crux of my dear cousin's delusion. The Drexel mine is of still of great value only in her mind. We all know that it's dry and worthless."

Mrs. Drexel asked, "And just how do you know that?"

"You've proved it yourself. Have you even found a trace of silver for the past decade?"

"No, I ain't."

"Case in point, Your Honor."

She snickered. "If that makes me crazy, then my Sam who founded this town, must have really been plumb crazy. He spent near fourteen years prospecting that mine before he made his first strike. So, I still got a few years to go, if I live that long."

"Yes, but there was silver there then."

"There is silver now."

"I'm sure you believe that, Mrs. Drexel, now Your Honor..."

Judge Mathis called for order in the court. "I'm sorry, Mrs. Drexel, but after Doc Jenkin's medical opinion and then what you yourself say, well, I'm afraid that the law allows me no alternative here..."

"But the..."

I stood and spoke up, "Excuse me, Your Honor."

"Now, now, see here. We're not going to allow any more interruptions."

"It's important, Your Honor."

"Who is this man, Doc?"

"Wade Maverick."

Judge Mathis smiled for the first time. "Maverick, the Red Gun?"

"Yes, may I speak, please?"

"Yes, Mr. Maverick, this court will be happy to hear you."

Thanks, Your Honor. I've been listening to this hearing and like Mr. Drexel says, all that matters is if there is still silver in the Drexel mine. If so, then Mrs. Drexel's actions wouldn't seem so strange, would they?"

"Well, no, I suppose not. She'd be protecting a valuable piece of land, but..."

"Yeah, well then perhaps maybe you ought to see this report here. You see, I took some ore samples from the Drexel mine over to the assayer's office this morning, and... Well, here's one of them."

"I'm afraid the court doesn't quite follow you, Mr. Maverick."

"If you'll just read that report, Your Honor."

"I see now...Hmm... Samples tested show a value of approximately one hundred and thirty dollars a ton."

Doc Jenkins arched an eyebrow, "A hundred and thirty dollars a ton?"

I answered, "Yeah, I figured they'd run a little higher, but I guess..."

Doc said, "May I see that, Judge?"

He put on his spectacles and read and reread slowly.

"I can't believe it!" he exclaimed. "Well, that's what it says, all right. One hundred and thirty dollars! This ore come from the Drexel?"

"Yeah, yeah, that's where it came from."

He raised the report over his head and shouted with glee. "Listen, listen everyone! My Lord! Bonnie's found silver again! For all we know, the whole town has been sitting on it, just like in the old days...Silver!"

Mr. Norris stood from the back of the courtroom. "But what about the railroad? You've got a contract with my company!"

"We don't need your railroad, Norris. Butterfield's got silver again!"

The crowd cheered wildly.

"Order! Order! Order!"

I added, "Now, maybe I wouldn't be too hasty, Doc."

Doc nodded. "Of course, Wade's right again. There's no possibility of bringing the line through the Drexel land now, but there is that other route."

Norris said, "It would cost my company more money...That might be arranged. Of course, I'll have to check with the main office."

Doc put the screws to him. "Oh, you would? Oh, that seems a shame. Too bad you can't sort of make the decision right now on the spot...You know, before another railroad hears about the silver and tries to beat you in here."

"Oh, well, on second thought, there really isn't any reason to delay the matter."

"If you'll just drop by my office, Dr. Jenkins, I'll fix up the contract tonight. Once you as Butterfield's mayor signs it, we'll give the order to begin construction on the other route."

"Very well, I think that'll be fine."

Judge Mathis called for order. "Well, I guess that takes care of everything, except Mrs. Drexel and the sanity hearing."

The crowd erupted once more.

"Order! Order! Everyone, now come to order."

Doc Jenkins proclaimed, "Well, there's no question now about Bonnie Drexel's sanity!"

Judge Mathis shrugged. "Is this your revised medical opinion?"

"In light of the facts, yes, Your Honor," Doc said as he turned to give Clint Drexel a hard look. "And I'm surprised at you, Mr. Drexel, a lawyer of your standing, pressing a complaint like this. Why Silver Bonnie Drexel is one of Butterfield's preeminent citizens. She always has been and always will be."

Judge Mathis cleared his throat. "Very well. This case is dismissed. Court is adjourned."

He slammed his gavel.

That was that.

Ironically, within ten minutes, the only people left in that courtroom were Mrs. Drexel and me. The funny thing was she was the only person in the room who showed no excitement about the silver.

She just kind of stared at me as her eyes teared up. And then the corners of her lips sort of wrinkled up into a mischievous smile.

Then, she took my hand in hers.

"Wade Maverick, you, you are one in a million!"

"Ma'am?"

"God bless you...You best get out of town before they find out. They'd tar and feather you for sure!"

"Well, just what are you talking about, Mrs. Drexel?"

Why, you think I didn't recognize that piece of ore?

"Well,..."

"I ought to. It's the first piece of ore my dear Sam brought up from the mine, from back in the day. I've been looking at it for thirty years."

"You don't say?"

"Them silver samples have been sitting on the top of my dresser ever since. You saw them last night. You knew they were souvenirs from the old days."

"Well, I'm no silver expert, ma'am, why couldn't they have been dug up this morning?"

"I'm not saying you lied, Wade. All you told them was that this was ore was from the Drexel mine. This is true. It's just a good thing they didn't ask you from when."

I smiled for the first time in days. "Yes, ma'am, it certainly is."

"You knew what you were doing. You also got the railroad coming through the other more costly route before they got wise."

"No, I wouldn't exactly say that, but under the circumstances, I think it's best Badger and I leave town."

I never returned to Butterfield, and it faded into ghost town oblivion.

It turns out the railroad never signed the contact and chose El Paso.

Life has a way of working out.

I trust you enjoyed *Red River Days*. The wanderings of Wade Maverick continue in *Frontier Echoes*.

Frontier Echoes

WHAT'S NEXT IN THE SERIES?

FRONTIER ECHOES

Escape back into the magnificent 19th century Texas Frontier.

These are the wanderings of an intrepid soul, Wade Maverick, from wild Wichita Falls, to tangling with outlaws in rough and tumble Tascosa and showdowns on

RED RIVER DAYS

a Comanche Moon...

Frontier Tales from Texas back in the day.

The fierce vaqueros of the Mexican border.

Wild and dangerous Wichita Falls.

Coming of age in bronc busting Lubbock.

Outlaws in rough and tumble Tascosa.

Keeping the peace in San Antonio.

Comanche Moon in the Texas Hill Country.

A living connection between America's past and present in the home of the free.

Frontier Echoes

Scan the QR Code below to order your copy of Frontier Echoes today.

FIND ME ON SOCIALS

Did you enjoy **Red River Days?**

Would it be crazy for me to ask for a quick Amazon review? It truly helps an indie author.

TEXAS TALES

WHISPERING WINDS

RED RIVER DAYS

FRONTIER ECHOES

DUST AND DREAMS

I'd like to invite you to join **"Wooden Nickels,"** my monthly newsletter! There are book extras, writing tips, contents, prizes, food for thought and the odd irresistible Tex-Mex recipe. It's also where I often seek your input on covers, character names, book titles, etc., and my list for new releases, special sales, and giveaways. **Join the fun.**

Website: akvyas.com
Facebook: @akvbook
Twitter: @akvyas18
Instagram: @akvyasauthor

About the Author

A. K. Vyas gave early promise of being nothing special whatsoever. He was born in the small New England village best known for the witch trials, then banished to Texas at a tender age. Being annoyingly well read for a Texan and exceptionally stubborn as a child, the smart money predicted a brief but clumsy career as a rodeo clown, while others foresaw an early death.

To everyone's intense disbelief, UC Berkeley made the mistake of admitting him, and he squeaked out a degree or two while doing silly acrobatic things in small planes. The Navy eventually decided it was safer for all parties involved (including the enemy) if he didn't fly jets. Like most wayward souls he ended up on Wall Street, a lifestyle interrupted from time to time by an occasional date, unless of course it was NCAA football season. (You can take a boy out of Texas but can't take Texas out of the boy.)

To date, his young family has survived two Category 5 hurricanes, and an infatuation with Tex-Mex cast-iron skillet recipes. Europe is currently home, and for unknown reasons, people on the street everywhere always ask him for directions. *The Eagle Feather* was his debut attempt at the ancient art of storytelling, and was written for his beautiful, perfect, athletic, and wonderful young son.

Writing has since evolved into a cathartic hobby.

ALSO BY A.K. VYAS

The Eagle Feather Saga

The Eagle Feather Saga is the unforgettable story of one boy's perilous journey to lead his tribe amidst the daunting challenges and savage splendor of prehistoric times.

Ballad of Shannon Dumas Series

Shannon is a frontier tale set amidst the backwoods bayous of antebellum Louisiana, the sprawling decadence of old New Orleans, and the mercilessly rugged Texas frontier.

Carnival Girls

Carnival Girls is a dark international thriller about a chilling serial killer who abducts coeds and the FBI agent trying to bring him to justice.

www.ingramcontent.com/pod-product-compliance
Lightning Source LLC
Chambersburg PA
CBHW022055050726
47591CB00002B/554